A Small Room with Trouble on

My Mind

And Other Stories

by

Mike Henson

For Leon and Sue —
Many thanks for the help,
support, advice, and faith. A lot of
this book is yours. I wish you
peace, strength, love.
Mike Henson

West End Press
Minneapolis, MN

Portions of this book have been previously published in: River City Review, Quindaro, Adena, Midwest Alliance, and Soupbean: An Anthology of Contemporary Appalachian Writing

Songs of which lines are quoted in this volume include:

The Fields Have Turned Brown—Carter Stanley
Got To Do My Time—Col. Jimmy Skinner
Dark Hollow—Traditional
Gold Watch and Chain—A.P. Carter (Carter Stanley?)
Ocean of Diamonds
Muleskinner Blues—Jimmie Rodgers and George Vaughan (BMI)
Rolling in My Sweet Baby's Arms—Charles Monroe (BMI)
Pretty Polly—Traditional
All the Good Times Are Past and Gone—Traditional
Short Life of Trouble

Photos: Barb Wolf
Book Design: Cathryn Stewart
Cover: Jim Dochniak

$5.00
ISBN 0-931122-31-7

Table of Contents

A Small Room with Trouble on My Mind

Short life of trouble
These few words to part
Short life of trouble, dear lord,
For a boy with a broken heart.

Pain grabs us, brother men...

Oh unfortunately, human men,
there's so much, brothers, so much to do.

—Vallejo

Some of the words (some) in this book and some of the events (only some) are from the lives of certain people, once friends of mine. I write this explanation so that it may be understood that this fiction (yes, fiction) has been written, not from bitterness, but from respect, from (yes, still) love. I wrote it to fulfill, in spite of some years and some pain, a promise I made years ago.

We were playing guitar in the kitchen, my friend and I. The children were racketing in the front room. The coffee went cold in our cups as we went from song to song, from breakdown to ballad.

"Now here's something for you," he told me. He picked a short turnaround. "It's a song I wrote years ago," he said. "At the time I wrote it, I meant every word." He sang,

> *It seems my whole life has been in vain*
> *Everything that I do somehow is wrong*
> *The sunshine never follows the rain*
> *And in a crowd I find myself alone*

Then, in higher pitch, the chorus:

> *Now I'm standing at the end of my world*
> *Looking back o'er my wasted past*
> *Thinking of the things that might have been*
> *If we'd live each newborn day as if the last*

He stopped in midchord, then leaned over his guitar and said, "That's all of it I can remember. It had an ending at one time, but for years I've tried to remember the rest.

"Now if you want to do something, write an end to that song. It's yours," he said. "Go ahead."

So I did:

I.

1.

The hand with the knife whets the blade across the watersmooth limestone step. Ten quick licks across the stone and the dark beak of the blade brightens. He tests it with his thumb.

The hollow wind carries a high note of long travel, pick and strum of pine and sycamore.

He picks up the branch of cherry that is thick as a man's arm. He turns it rippled and red as muscle as he strips back the bark, pulling loose wide curls of black and red that drop around his shoes and onto the stone step and into the grass of the yard.

The veins of his hands darken like broad rivers on a map.

He chips and slices with the wind in his ear until he has it in rough banjoneck shape. Then he eyes it end to end.

Already, he can hear the lonesome note that will live across it.

● ● ●

Low voice of the shivering wind: Soft crack of the porchboards as he leans over his work: Low slack sound of the newstrung string: Tuning twang tuningtwang tuning twaiiing: Right.

Chordstroke:

Sharp voice of the stretched hide and its wooden frame.

He plays:
> *Polly pretty Polly come go along with me*
> *Polly pretty Polly come go along with me*
> *Before we get married some pleasure we'll*

See his fingers slide along the neck: Hear the bent and hurting notes:
> *Willie oh Willie I'm fraid of your ways*
> *Willie oh Willie I'm fraid of your ways*
> *The way you been ramblin*

Pine-shaped wind and creaking porchboard: Straying voice of hide and woodframe and wirestrain:

> *will lead me astray*

4

2.

East Kentucky, 1938

The dew was cold on the faces of the boy and the man. It lay dark on the heavy leaves of the trees that climbed the mountains on both sides of them and on the tin roofs of the double row of houses behind them and on the waiting railroad tracks that gleamed with the first white blade of morning. The boy's eye followed the long steel rail to where it bent around the mountain and disappeared like a grim smile.

His father pulled the gold watch and chain from the breast of his overalls and popped it open with his thumb. The boy listened. He listened each time the man pulled the watch, big as a silver dollar, out of the breast pocket of his overalls. The sound he listened for was the triphammer sound of its ticking, as if someone within labored at a rail. He could hear it now, a loud, regular, complicated sound, made up of the work of the hundred gears and springs and linkages. He could hear it, even above the iron sound of strain as the railroad engine, on the far side of the mountain, worked toward them. But only rarely could he see the face of the watch and he strained now and could not see the antique numbers or the gold sweep of the hands.

The train whistled hoarsely and his father said, "Right on the nail." He snapped the watch shut and stuck it back into the breast of his overalls. He reached down to pick up his lunch pail and drew one last time on his cigarette, then threw the butt to the ground.

The boy stepped over to stomp it out. The man watched him, but said nothing.

The train came around the mountain. The boy could see its headlamp swimming toward them through the trees like a bright fish through the weeds of a pond.

"Right on time," his father said. "Dead on it." Then he bent down his cap, stooped to his lunch pail, struck a match against a rough corner of it, and held the flame to the point of his lamp. The carbide flickered, then billowed out a blue circle of light onto the dark ground.

The train had cleared the woods now and they could see the black heaps of the coal cars glinting in the new light and they could see the great wings of steam that the engine raised as it slowed for a curve. Then hissing and growling like a great iron bear, it was on them.

His father stepped close to the tracks and he was swallowed by steam and sound. Clatter Clatter Clatter Clatter. The boy saw the carbide beam nod in time with the pounding of the iron wheel against a link in the tracks. His father looped the wire of his lunch pail over his shoulder, then counted four more times the beat of the rail: Clatter Clatter Clatter Clatter. Then, as fear rose up in the belly of the boy like a trapped bird, the man fixed his beam on the ladder of a coal car, followed it with a slow turn of his head to keep the light on it, then suddenly threw up one hand to grab a ladder-rung, swung himself up onto the flank of the car, and hung on.

If the man looked back, the boy didn't see. The carbide light winked out and the train worked along the scimitar tracks into the blindness of the mountain.

3.

The house they visited looked as if it had been blown into the side of the mountain. The grey shingles sloped up with the hillside so that the peak of the roof was lost in the bluegrey stitching of the pines. The barn lay further back, up a red strip of lane, and the sheds and outbuildings were set in the yard at random like knots of grey lumber. A wire fenceline fronted the yard to keep the cattle out and crossed a little run that shared the road and lost itself in the woods running up the opposite hill. The wind had scattered leaves, ancient cans, newspapers, shattered packing boxes, odds and ends of rope, cloth, paper through the yard. Each of them was greying, rusting or rotting so that they merged by color and decomposition with the grass and earth along the hem of the fences and in the corners of the woodpile and the outbuildings.

They had walked a long hollow road to this house. "Come on boys," his father said to his brother and to him, "I got me a banjo to sell." He carried the banjo in a feed sack on his shoulder. It was a road they had not walked before. It ran alongside, and sometimes over, and sometimes through a little run, crossed it on narrow plank bridges, or shared the same bed with it. It was a long silent road, for after it left the main road from the coal camp, few houses faced it, and several were empty.

Children in the yards or men in the fields would stop their work or play as they passed, silent, uncurious, giving as gesture a nod or small wave of the hand.

Their father walked with his hands in his pockets and his jacket open to the October wind. He whistled, but the whistling was lost on that wind that came down from the ridgetops with a cold smell of ash.

Their own place was close to the road. No matter where they lived, it was always close to a road. Each time they got ready for a move, they knew they could expect a place near a hard road and a yard with a space for the car—even when they didn't have one.

At this point of the hollow, the wind held itself in the ridgetops. A man stood in the darkness and cream of the porch. His shout, *yoh*, a brief non-word that carried acknowledgement, welcome, and warning, floated down to them like a hawk.

"They tell me you're looking for a banjo," his father shouted back. The man waited as they came through the gate, crossed the yard and stopped at the porch steps. "I'm lookin," the man said. Their father sat down, unbagged the banjo, and handed it to the man to tune it. He studied it, placed it to his eye to sight it like a gunbarrel, took it through the first bars of half a dozen tunes, then put it down.

The man and their father talked a while longer. Neither one mentioned the banjo. The tunes the man had played still shimmered in the boy's ear, like the low tremble of a branch once someone has bent it then let it go. He and his brother hunkered at the bottom of the steps. He closed his eyes and tried to hear the tunes again, but they were lost in the little wind that sifted

7

through the yard grass. They were not the tunes his father played. He saw that his father had listened closely, but they were not the quick dancing tunes that his father played.

There was a woman, watching. He could see her white figure in the darkness of the doorway, but she made no offer to come onto the porch until their father said, "Well sing one for us, will you?"

The man looked back at the doorway and the woman came out and sat on the porch between the men. Their father didn't try to tease her, as he did so many of the women.

The man started the song. In his lone voice, it was like one of the slow melodic songs that he heard in church. The woman watched at a point just in front of the man's face and when she spotted the right word, she leaned forward, hawklike, almost as if she could see it and seize it, and joined him. The two changing and counter-changing voices were a shock to him, something that, even if it was not new, was something he had never before fully heard. The crossing sounds, floating over the hollow wind, frightened him, for he felt fragile and uplifted like a floating bird, so light as to be almost bodiless, and became bodiless, unprotected.

Why had he never felt this before? And why was this fear one that he did not want to release?

Trellis and vine, their voices, he followed them until they stopped. He remembered none of the talk that followed. He remembered that his father left behind the banjo, though he did not remember any money. He remembered the troublesome wind that followed them back to the road.

He remembered the strong lines in the face of the woman.

4.

That's the bitter one, she thought. She was watching him where he stood in the yard, leaning at the gate, peering through the pickets as if he could throw his eye through the narrow slot and drag the rest of him behind it into the cindergrey dust of the road. He was staring after the car that was now half a mile down the road and long out of sight, but he would stare after it, she knew, until the last of the road dust had settled onto the roadbed, the tips of the fencepickets, the cabineaves and windowsills, the melons of the garden, and further off, where his long eye leaned, onto the leaves of the trees at the roadbend where the car had disappeared.

He'll never say it out, but the hurt goes deep in him, she thought. The others get hurt, they'll fight with it til they don't feel it so much anymore. But he'll carry that hurt with him just like a pet that he'd carry in his hands.

A coal truck battered past them and the cloud of dust it raised overpowered the last whisps of the car's dust. The boy pulled back from the fence and the blinding truckdust cloud. He stood on tiptoe to see over the fence, but its thick nest of shrubs and the pale heads of the late summer grasses blocked him.

He rocked back on his heels, still staring at the coal dust billows that already were settling back into the roadbed. The noise of the truck was already droning out like a trapped housefly. She watched him. He stuck his hands down into his pockets and stared first at his shoes, then at a stiff tuft of grass, a broken-rung rocking horse, the spade still standing halfway down the potato row, and finally, back to the road where the dust now carpeted the empty highway.

He might have gone back to the gate to look again. He might have gone to the garden. He might have mounted his broken horse. But she had turned back to the kitchen, matching in her mind the coming bills to the checks that would not come, pondering her stores of beans, cornmeal, and the undug potatoes, and trying to recall the signs that told if a winter would be hard.

5.

Randall Martin:

Now my dad, he wasn't no talker at all. We'd be cuttin wood in the hottest part of the summer and layin it up in the yard. And I'd ask him, "Dad, why are we cuttin all this wood now?" And all he'd say was, "Wait till winter." And that's all he ever would say about it. Sure enough, come winter, I saw what he meant. It took six months for him to get his message across.

Whatever he was thinkin, he'd keep it to himself. He'd be settin around the house, not sayin a word, and all of a sudden, he'd get up and pick up an axe and go out into the woods and go tappin that axe against the trees. For the sound of it. And when he got the one he wanted, he'd cut it down. Before too long, he'd made it into a chair or a rifle stock or a banjo. He made these fretless banjoes. Cover it with any kind of hide, coon, possum, anything.

You know, we used to keep these frames for stretching hides out on the porch. We had em different sizes, for a coon, a possum, squirrel or whatever. And we had a dog that would look at that stretcher we'd set out, and whatever size it was, he'd go out and catch an animal to fit it.

Well, one day we put the ironing board out there by mistake. That dog looked at it, took off, and never did come back.

But you know, Dad was about like that old dog for takin off, and he gave Mom a pretty rough way to go. He'd take off whenever he felt like it and he'd stay gone as long as he cared to. One day he stood up and said, "I'm goin fishin." And he didn't come back for two whole years.

But he come back with that same pole and a stringer full of fish.

6.

The first time he ever saw a piano up close was when they moved out of the coal camp to the town where they had a courthouse and they had a school with six rooms and six teachers. He'd had to wait in the classroom of his older brother while his older brother helped the teacher, and as he waited he was drawn to the tall box, black as a coffin and grinning with music.

When he got up by it, close enough to reach it, he wondered if he would get in trouble if he made just one note by mashing on a key. He'd seen it done in a movie. He looked around him. The teacher had gone out in the hall and his brother was cleaning the blackboard. He could try just one note if he did it soft. He picked one of the white ones, near the middle. He pushed slowly and softly, and it made no sound but a soft wooden rattle. He pushed it again, harder this time, and it sang a note this time. Too loud, he thought. He turned quickly to see who might have heard. But his brother went on with his cleaning and the two girls dusting tables were giggling softly to each other about some other thing.

What makes the notes? he wondered. Silently pushing the key again he could feel through his finger the workings of the wooden pieces that were jointed like bones. What do they do? he wondered. How do they make a noise? He looked behind him again. No one was watching, so he lifted the door above the keys and saw the sheltered strings, pegs, and hammers. He pushed the note once more and saw the felt head of a hammer lean forward out of its rank to peck like a hen at one of the dark strings. The string shimmered and sang, louder this time so that he looked behind him again.

His brother, stacking erasers now, looked over to him in a bored way. The girls were still bent over their giggling work.

He slowly closed the door and stepped back to see what else there was to look at, and his eye went to the top shelf where a triangular wooden box sat. A narrow strip of bars was riveted to it so that the strip stood straight up from the base of the triangle. The top half of the box was open. The writing on the label on the front was in the fancy antique letters like those on the cover of a Bible.

11

He stood on the piano bench to look closer and peered into the opening. Nothing he saw made any sense to him. The inside of the box was dark. Standing on tiptoe, his hands bracing him against the top of the piano, he peered closer down into the opening until his nose just grazed the upright metal shaft.

TALK. TALK. TALK. TALK. In horror, he jerked back. The TALK metal TALK shaft TALK had TALK started TALK to TALK rock TALK back TALK and TALK forth, louder than a voice, regular as a clock, but faster. TALK TALK TALK unstoppably rocking. He could see no switch, no way to shut it off. The sound TALK TALK TALK TALK was magnified by the silence of the unwhispering girls. Without turning he could see clear as sight his brother with the blackboard rag in his hand forming in thought the words, *that little sonofabitch.*

But he was unprepared for the shadow that reached across him toward the clocklike thing. The shadow had an arm, and he knew by its size and by the bright silver watch on its wrist that it was the teacher.

She had stopped it. He heard the girls' soft whisper and heard his brother's angry blackboard rag slap the floor, and he already heard the story that his brother would tell at home. *You can't take him nowhere. He won't let nothin alone.*

"It's a metronome," the teacher was saying. "It helps you keep time when you're playing the music."

But the whisper of the girls and the slap of his brother's rag had burned out whatever other words the woman spoke. He had turned with his small fists doubled so hard that they hurt, thinking, *Let them try to say something.* But the girls had turned their embarrassed faces back to their work and his brother was reaching for his disgusted blackboard rag.

He looked up at the teacher whose puzzling face was stopped on an unheard question. She would teach him the mystery of that box, he knew, but it would only be while that whispering and disgust mocked him from behind.

He made one more powerless turn about the room and ran out before the tears flashed across his face.

12

7.

The fever blew in on him like a hard rain. A rasping wind festered through his throat and funneled into his belly and tangled his long rope of bowel. The spaces of his head were filled with the backwaters of the storm, and in the cabin of each cell burned a furnace against the hard wind. It burned in each bead of his brain, in every string of muscle, and in each tissue of the walls and channels of his growing heart.

Rheumatic fever, the doctor said. He lay in his bed for six long weeks, unable to move his legs, cursing his immobility under his breath so as not to let his mother hear, but cursing with all the strength he had so that he fell asleep at odd hours of the day or night, exhausted as if he had been in daylong labor. Then he lay awake in the sleepless night, thinking, Now what if I'm a cripple for all my life?

From the kitchen, an endless clock told him of each sleepless second. The heavy sound of his brother's breathing grew up around him like tall grasses. The roots of the grasses embraced his buried legs and the seed-heavy tops of the grasses scratched at his face. They forced pollen under the lids of his eyes. The leaves of the grasses whispered at his ears, as he waited in tearless agony for the morning, his curses silent and constant as the beat of his heart.

•   •   •

Then one day I got up and I could walk. A little wobbly, but I could get across the room. That coal camp doctor said he couldn't figure it out. It wasn't in none of his books.

I begun to get my strength back, little bit by bit, and in a week or two I was strong as ever, workin ever day and eatin the legs right off the table, just like I always done.

I been workin a full day's work, you see, ever since I was twelve. When I was just a boy I'd spend a ten or twelve hour day on a tractor or cuttin wood or workin with a hoe.

13

I never did go into the mines, though. I hated the mines. I hated those little coal camps. A coal camp is a dirty little town. There's just something about those mines and those dirty little towns I never liked. Coal dust all over everything. You couldn't keep it out. Mom would wipe it off the windowsill even in winter when all the windows would stay closed.

It was better when we lived up in Indiana. Dad would take a factory job in one little town or another and we'd pack up there behind him. That's where I first began to work on my own, for the farmers around there, tryin to help Mom out, tryin to learn whatever I could.

I always watched whenever I seen somebody workin on somethin that I hadn't seen before. I'd watch just as close as I could til I thought I knew it and then I'd try it myself. I couldn't set still for school, but I could set for an hour to watch somebody do a valve job.

That's how I learned to play the guitar: watchin. I watched the Gene Autry movies to learn my first chords. I'd look to see how he held his fingers on the frets, and then I'd fix my fingers that same way and I'd walk all the way home with my fingers set in that chord til I could get hold of the guitar to try it out. And you figure, most of these country songs, there's three chords. Well, it'd take me three movies just to learn one song.

And I learned a lot from the people who would come to the house. My dad knew some of the early Opry stars, even, and if we'd be livin in Kentucky, all sorts of music people would visit. One old boy, he played the banjo, he had only one arm, and I don't know how he did it except that you'd swear he got his foot in there somehow.

Me and some of the younger ones around, we'd go out to a barn and play, whatever few songs we knew. Some songs, whenever I hear em now, all I can smell is hay and cowshit.

I played some nights til it was almost light and I had to work the next day, and I'd lay down for an hour when I couldn't play no more, and then I'd get up and go out in them fields and work twelve hours and come back in hopin I wouldn't even see that guitar. But then I'd see it and there I'd be, workin at it til my fingers would bleed and I'd cry from the pain.

Now if you're gonna take up learnin to play the guitar, I'll tell you. Forget those books. Just hit those strings. You see, you can't just know it in your head. You've got to know it in your hands. You use your eyes to read a book. But you use your fingers to read those strings, and if you work at it right, they'll tell you what you want to know. Your eye can't tell you and your mind can't tell you what you're gonna do with those strings. If you have to stop to think about it, you'll lose your timing. You've got to know it in your hands. You don't really know somethin unless you know it in your hands.

I got to where I knew all the styles in bluegrass and country. Jimmy Rodgers and the Carter Family were some of my favorites. But the ones that meant the most to me was the Stanley Brothers, Ralph and Carter. Ralph still sings that high lonesome sound. But Carter died a few years back, drank himself to death. He could play a tune on that guitar that could put tears in the eyes of a hardened killer or it could make the dead walk, then he'd say "Wait til you hear what I can do with my gloves off."

I learned all those styles, but I always tried to do it my own way. Dad would say, "Why don't you try to pick like so and so?" Well I didn't want to play like so and so or anybody else. I wanted to make my own style. Nobody else's. I can't take up somebody else's way of playin and still be me. Can I? Tell me how I can.

Well I'd work pretty hard at it for awhile. Then for two weeks or a month I might drop it altogether. I might go out to a movie in town or fish or go on a drunk. I might drop it for three or four months, even. The folks might not think too much the first night, but as the days went on they'd get sort of uneasy. They never would say nothin, but you could tell they were bothered. Then once I begun to playin again, they'd sort of relax. Like they'd been afraid of what I might do if I didn't have a guitar in my hands.

Part of why I'd quit was that I would know I'd gone as far as I could with it right then. I'd pushed myself to where I couldn't learn what I wanted to learn, couldn't do what I knew I could do, and I just had to get away from it.

And part of it was that I'd get afraid. Like that guitar was in control of me, and it was pushin me. People too, they like to see you stay with just one thing, so they can hold you in one place in their minds and say, He's a guitar picker or he's a welder or she's a waitress, and they think they've got you where they want you.

So I had to put it down. Just so I could know I was still me.

8.

When he stepped into the dark hall, he saw a dim line of light under his mother's door. So she knew. He hesitated. He already had his suitcase with him. He'd had it hidden beneath his bed. But the guitar was in the hall, by the coatrack, and there was no way to get it without bending the floorboards or bumping the suitcase against a wall or making some kind of noise. He stared at the narrow strip of light and the smoky grain of the floorboards, listening for any sign until he realized that she intended to make no sign, that she was not awake to catch him or to talk him out of going. She might be reading her Bible or sewing or fretting, but she would not pace the floor or come out to stop him or tell him goodbye. She had created an awesome, glasslike silence. She had nothing to say that was not said by that slim bar of light.

What could he do? It was not even that she had created an argument. For him, leaving was necessary as breath or heartbeat, yet that slim bar of light on the floor was her denial. Her pride, he knew, would let her speak no other way. He felt he owed her, at least, his silence. The expected floorboard creaked, but he was able to pull the guitar from its corner without thumping it on the wall. The only further sounds he made were his steps on the stairs and the click of the door as he shut it.

9.

Now I've had many jobs in my time, startin back when I was a boy workin for the farmers around. I been pullin my own weight all this time.

When I was about seventeen, though, I was crazy to go in the army. Even when I wasn't old enough yet I'd hang around the Post Office, actin old. I went in after Mom signed the papers and a year later I was in Korea. I fought there and I froze there. It was an ugly place to be. After Korea I stayed on another four years, mostly workin as a mechanic. For a while they had us stationed in Greenland, and while I was there we got ice-locked in and they couldn't get us any supplies, so we lived three weeks on pepper soup and crackers.

Greenland was pretty cold, but it wasn't the worst. I almost froze to death one night right in Pennsylvania. I'd got out on leave from Fort Bragg, North Carolina and I left there in eighty degree weather with a short-sleeve shirt on. I got a ride as far as Pittsburgh and the temperature started to drop. And for some reason I couldn't get a ride out of this little place just outside Pittsburgh. I don't know if it's just that people's hearts get harder once the weather gets colder or if they figured by me just standin there in my shirtsleeves I must of just escaped from somewhere. But the cars, what few there was, just kept goin on by and the weather got colder and colder til finally I just had to start walkin to keep from freezin to death. I didn't even have a suitcase with me cause I had everything I needed back at home.

The sun begun to go down and I got real scared. They say that hell isn't just fire and flame. It's freezing and ice. There wasn't a hand would turn to help me, and I started to give up. When you're out there like that, you feel like the whole world is pointin its finger at you and sneerin. And then you begin to feel yourself disappear, like you're just made of snow. A trucker finally picked me up, and I hated him, cause warmin up made me hurt.

But after I got out of the army I took a truck drivin job. I hauled new cars, furniture, anything. I even worked for awhile runnin from Texas up to up north with a load of fencepost holes that they cut up out of used oil wells.

I've tended gas stations, run a milk route, tended bar, drove cab, run a parts desk. But mostly I've done machinist work. That's where my best money's been.

I got started at that one day in Fort Wayne Indiana when I hired on in a place and he asked me if I could run a lathe. I'd never seen one before, but I said, hell yea, so he took me in there and left me alone with it. In about half an hour's time I had it figured out.

After that, I never did fear to run any kind of machine. They're made for you to run them. You just have to study them out. If you let a machine worry you, you'll let that machine run you.

I don't let no machine run me. Nor nothin else either.

10.

All that lay shelved in the bins of memory: Years full of the clatter of machinery and the rough voices of motors. Battle noise of Korea. The slow daylong dance of the Greenland sun. Nights wired with neon, voices trellising around those lights in lonesome harmony. The small Indiana towns, islands in the cornswept fields. The hard streets of Cincinnati, Louisville, Covington. Coal camp towns split by pocked roads that cursed with the weight of the coal trucks. Highway nights where the wind wrapped itself around the house and made one single sound with the cars that dove behind their headlights into the darkness.

The ancient, stacked box apartments where the walls were made of ears:

"I'm leaving," she said. The baby was wrapped in its blankets. The girl was trussed in her jacket and a heavy scarf.

"I don't know if you can even understand what I'm tryin to tell you," she said.

He thought: *I should be tryin to talk to her. I should be tryin to cry.* But no hint of tears or sorrow or regret or guilt came to him, only the dark wave of the alcohol in his veins, the grain of beer in his nostrils.

"You're right," he said.

"What?"

"You're right. I don't even know what you're...". He took a deep breath so as to try to straighten out the slurring of his words. "I don't know what you're trying to tell me."

He knew nothing. He almost laughed to think of it. He tried, but he couldn't know a thing.

He was fishing on a boat in black waters where the waters made no sound, where the sky was ringed with the last light, and his line held a silver bait that would catch nothing.

"You're laughin at me," she said. She was pulling on her coat, but stopped with the coat still limp across her shoulders. "Goddam you, you're laughin at me."

He saw her whirl around for the shelf with the coat still hanging loose from her shoulders, and the first thing her hands touched was the cereal box. Then, through a shower of cornflakes, he saw her grab the toaster.

Both of them hit him. He was not sure where or how bad, but he knew that he turned to face her, and that a black tide of anger was rising up in him as she grabbed a fork and flung it at him. It end-overended into his belly and stuck there, humming like a tuning fork.

Stunned, amused, he sat back and stared at the ring of blood that formed on his t-shirt. When finally he looked up from the spreading oval of blood, she was gone.

She didn't feel gone. She didn't even hurt where she had hit him nor even where the fork still stood out from his belly like a silver perch.

•   •   •

When he woke, the blood had stiffened into a brown disk around the fork. He touched the end of it and it fell out of his flesh with a sharp pain like a bandage being ripped away. The pain dove inward through his belly and sickened him so that he leaned forward to violently heave out the soured sack of his stomach. He heaved himself down onto his knees, heaved the night's drinking out of him like a movie running backwards so that he was becoming steadily more sober and there was nothing more to heave but nothingness and hurt.

When the heaving finally slowed to a weak dry bleating, he stood to pull himself out of a sea of vomit, walked on uneasy legs to the bathroom, stripped off his soiled shirt and trousers, and held his head under the bathtub faucet until the smell left him.

He went to the bedroom and changed into fresh clothes. Then, because he could still smell the sourness, he dashed his face with aftershave.

My hand's shakin, he noticed as he tried to steady the bottle back on the dresser. *It don't feel like it's shakin, but it's sure enough shakin.* The shaking hand tilted the bottle across a hair brush and spilt it. The perfumed smell spread over him like a defeat. The lotion pooled around the base of the alarm clock. For the first time he heard it ticking. Four O Eight in the morning. Each tick was sudden and final. Just so many. Four O Nine.

The smell of perfume and vomit was smothering him and he tried to wave the smell away. When it wouldn't leave he began to hurry. He pulled the guitar case from below the bed and a small suitcase from the closet. *She left me these at least,* he thought. Then he stuffed each of them as full as it would go, counted out the change still in the dresser drawer, and started toward the stairs.

II.

1.

Rosetta Martin:

I was born in a coal camp too, but it wasn't quite the hardship that he seen. He won't talk about it, about the hardship I mean, but I've heard his mother and his brothers tell of it, and I know that they had it hard.

We was poor, but we never did go hungry. And that's the difference. I've known people who went hungry when they were a child, and it does somethin to them. They've got an anger, deep down inside em, ever after that. They can be real nice people, some of the best. But they'll carry that anger with em all their lives, like a birthmark. It just lays there waitin. And they might hurt you. Or they might hurt themselves.

That's why I've always worked hard to keep my kids from goin hungry. I don't ever want em to go hungry for their health and all of course, but there's more to it. I don't want em to carry that kind of anger with em.

Where I grew up, it was a coal camp, like I say, but we didn't have it real bad like some. We had just a small place. Daddy worked in the mines and so did my older brother. And it was alright til the mines started closin down and Daddy lost his job. He said, "Aint nothin here to wait for." So he hopped on the Greyhound for Covington, figuring we could follow once he got settled. Well that didn't work out too good. So he come back down here and odd-jobbed it til we got to doin pretty good. At least we never did go hungry.

Music was always part of our life. Me and my sisters would wake up singin. It could be any old kind of thing, gospel or country or bluegrass. I remember hearin Ernest Tubb singin "Walkin the Floor over You" and thinkin that meant that somebody was down underneath the floorboards where he was walkin. We had an old Ford out in the yard that, whenever we'd hear a song on the radio that we wanted to learn, we'd take a pencil and write it out, quick as we could, on the body of that car. Then we'd lean our elbows against the hood of that car where we'd written that song and we'd practice, just making the trees ring.

My brothers was allowed to roam around pretty much as they wanted, but me and my sisters, we were always confined pretty much to the house unless it was to school or to church. Of course, Mama needed us to help with the cookin and the washin and the cannin and all. But it hurts a person to be shut up that way. They don't learn as much of the ways of the world and they have a harder time learnin to get on in life. At least I did.

But even with that we would slip away as much as we could, me and my sisters. I was a little slower to take up on it—being the youngest and everything, but once I made up my mind to go, sooner or later I was gone. Wasn't nothin could hold me.

I don't mean to say we went anywhere real bad. We'd slip off to a barn dance or a church social. And we might stay an hour or two to flirt with the boys. It wasn't what you'd call runnin around, but my Daddy didn't hold by it. Still today, he tries to tell me that all my trouble in life started right there—slippin off to barn dances and church socials.

And he might be right, cause that's how I met Randall, and he's been most of my trouble in life. I don't see how it would of made any difference though, I don't. Cause all of them stay-at-home mousey types that always minded their folks and never did anything wrong, they all ended up hard-luckin it just as bad as anybody else with their men. Only difference is that they're usually so sorry that they can't help themselves when they need to and they head right back for home first time things get bad. Me, I wouldn't look back home for help if it killed me. I'd die first, after the way Daddy's ragged me all these years. I've bar-maided and waitressed and babysat and picked pills in a pill factory and sorted tomatoes in a canning factory and I've been on welfare and a few other things besides, but I swear I'd pick garbage, I would, before I'd beg off somebody that's run me down the way he's done.

He'd just use it to try to get me to admit I was wrong. I love my Daddy, but that's a fault in him, to try to make somebody believe something just to get some help, and I can't take that kind of help.

And I might of been wrong. In fact, I probably was. But I'd make up my mind and I couldn't back down after that.

You see, I'd met him at one of those socials, and he was singin at that time with a bluegrass group that his brother'd put together.

23

Mostly, he played lead guitar. You could see him workin up and down the neck of that thing and you could hear the fancy finger work he was addin in. Most bluegrass groups then, they didn't have that much real guitar playin. Just guitar for the rhythm. Only the groups like the Stanley Brothers would do a lot of guitar, and of course the Stanley Brothers was his favorites.

Carter Stanley was the one. He played a lot around the low notes and it would sound so sad. They sung a lot of sad songs, gospel tunes, hearts and flowers, songs about mother and dad, home, love. They were from away back in the hills of Virginia and you could tell it by the words of their songs. You'd hear them sing something like this:

> The waters rose high on the river at midnight
> I sat on the shore to grieve and to cry
> The woman I love she left me this morning
> With no one to love me or kiss me goodnight

and it would be in that high and lonesome two-part or three- or four-part harmony that would make you shiver.

The first time I ever saw him or heard him sing it was a Stanley Brothers song. It was at a dance in a schoolhouse. They'd played a lot of dance numbers, square dance numbers. You know the kind of thing they play. And he'd not sung a lick the whole night long. Then the lead singer, the one who'd been talkin and gabbin the whole night long, he says, And now we're gonna persuade my brother Randall to come on up front and sing one. And it was like they'd shot him. He didn't want to move. He shook his head and you could see his lips move: Nooo, he said. But his brother pushed him on and he got up there in the middle of em and he kind of looked around him and grinned for a second. Then he begun to sing:

> I left my old home way back in the mountains
> Mother and Dad said son don't go wrong

It's the one with the chorus that goes like this:

> Son don't go astray, is what they both told me
> Remember that love forgot can be found
> But now they're both gone, this letter just told me
> For years they've been dead, the fields have turned brown

Well it just took my breath away.

24

Everybody else, they were polite, but what they wanted was somethin they could dance to, so there wasn't but a little bit of clappin. He just turned away real sober lookin like he hadn't wanted to be up there anyway and this just had embarrassed him. Well I hadn't even thought to clap, I was so winded by what I'd heard. But I didn't want him to think there wasn't somebody that liked it, so I started pumpin my hands together like some old drunk in a bar, I guess. And when he heard that, he gave that little grin again.

Well I didn't clap long, cause right away I felt embarrassed at bein so loud all by myself. And I got embarrassed by the way he raised his eyebrow to another man in the band. And that man winked. I couldn't stand it after that. I felt like, you know, I had cheapened myself.

You see, at that time, any time a girl showed herself too forward she could get considered, you know, a tramp. And I know that's just what Daddy would of called me if word had got back to him.

So I just shrunk down in my chair when he sang the next one. And I didn't look at him once again the rest of the night. And when I left I didn't want to see him ever again, I was so embarrassed.

And I didn't see him again for another six months. My sisters and all my friends all teased me about him, but I pretended I didn't care. People said he was travelin at the time lookin for work. That was the fifties, you see, and it was fairly good times in other parts, but not in the coal country. Ever little bit you'd see some family packed up to go. And off they'd go, north to some factory town. And their house would just go to waste from the weather and the boys breakin the windows.

I remember how I come to realize just what was happenin. You know how it is when you live right with somethin and never even notice what's goin on. Well, one night, right along dark, I went out to set on the porch, and right there, out of ever house I could see, the one to my right and the one to my left and the two or three across from me, not a one was lived in. And ever one was just an old unpainted company house that people had bought just before the mine closed. It got darker and darker, and all those grey houses just seemed to shudder and to moan from inside those black windows. And even though I knew there were my people right there in the house and there were people just up the street and just down the street, I couldn't help but feel I was alone and abandoned like an orphan child.

And it got darker and the lights went on in the house, so I couldn't see the abandoned houses all go black with the darkness, but I couldn't bring myself to leave, for I felt like those abandoned houses and me, we were children lost and abandoned together and I could almost hear them speak. I could feel those houses dyin. Houses die, just like people. They live a certain life, and then they just don't live no more. They die. Or they're killed. And when a person dies, there's a moment, just as that person passes into death, you can feel it, and you can feel yourself bein swept along with it. And it's not a frightful feelin. It's somethin that you share with that person, a feelin that you're right bein carried along together to some dark and unknown place, and that person's goin just ahead of you. And you wish them all the courage and strength they'll need to face whatever's there.

That's how I felt, sittin in the dark with those empty houses all around me.

Well, Daddy had stayed on at the mine even with the short hours, where even the men they had kept on had only two or three days work a week, til finally they were just down to just one or two and he said, I aint takin no more of this and he caught that Greyhound north, lookin for a job. Mommy and us kids moved to Hazard where we had some kin.

And that's where I met Randall. His family was pretty well known around there, but he'd been gone to the army and been married before and had been truck drivin and workin in Indiana and here and there, so he was a kind of mystery to everone about. That should of made me wonder, and it did, but that made him all the more interesting to me. And I reckon I felt sorry for him too, for he never seemed to be close to anybody. Not that he was poor company or felt sorry for himself. He'd always be crackin a joke or tellin some big kind of a lie. But he'd always seem to be pullin himself out of some sad mood to tell that joke, just like he pulled himself out of that bashful mood to sing that song.

Well, to make a long story short, he began to seriously courtin me and I was playin him along, not really knowin my own mind in it, til one day, Daddy come back all disgusted from tryin to find work up there in the city. I reckon he did find some kind of work up there, for he'd send money back and he had some money saved once he'd come back. What kind of work I never did know, for he never would talk about it. Not to us kids at least. I'm sure he told

Mommy what it was like up in the city and what he had done there, but he never did tell us. And that made in me a kind of fear of the city, knowin it made Daddy feel so awful he wouldn't even talk about it and that he spent days after he come back just sittin on the porch, angry-like, clenchin up his fists.

And in a few days he went back to odd-jobbin, maybe paintin a house or haulin coal or tradin, and he didn't spend any more time just settin. But he was still pretty angry-lookin and not really payin attention to anything other than to where he could get a job. but I guess it finally came around to him that I was courtin, for one night he said to me, "Let's take a look at what sort of fish you caught."

Well I knew then that I had to bring him up to the house, so I made a date for him to come up there, which was hard to do cause he didn't like to be told what to do and he sure didn't want to be inspected. But somehow or another I finally got him up there.

It was sort of like a standoff. There was somethin between them that I couldn't understand. I started out to say "Daddy this is..." and he stopped me cold and said, "I know." And then he called Mommy to bring him some coffee and talked with me and him for about half an hour or so. And never did look at him once. Just looked out past Randall's shoulder through the window to that little rutted street where we lived.

Well finally Randall got up to leave and I told him goodbye and went on to wash the winders or somethin like that and Daddy called me. "Girl," he said. And I came into the kitchen. "Girl, that man aint never gonna amount to nothin and if you stay by him you'll be buyin yourself nothin but a life of trouble."

I said, "How can you say that? '

"I reckon I said it."

"I mean, what makes you think he's so damn worthless?" I guess he was ready for me to get mad, for he didn't even care that I cussed.

"Where's he workin?" he asked.

I said, "He aint working any one place. He just works around, like everybody else." Which he did. He was makin some money fixin cars and playin at socials and repairin houses and so on, which if you didn't work in the mines was all you could do.

"Well why did he leave a good job up in Indiana to come down here and live when he could be makin good money and makin somethin of himself?"

Well I had to think hard about that for a minute. I didn't know. But then it hit me, why hell Daddy, you done the same damn thing ...and I almost said it. Except that I knew that if I did I might not be here now to tell of it.

And I got real confused. For, except for what I almost said, I didn't really have an answer to that one. There he was, odd-jobbin and playin music when he could of been up in Indiana makin good money and gettin himself ahead. Of course, I didn't care, for if he'd been in Indiana I couldn't never have met him. But I couldn't say that, so I just stood there sort of bitin my tongue and trying hard to think, til finally, Daddy, he said, "Well, since you aint got nothin to say for yourself, I want you to think on what I said. That man aint worth the powder it'd take to blow him up, and if you was to take up with him you'd be signin yourself over to a poor miserable life."

Then, before I could get riled up enough to walk off on him like I intended to do, he turned his back on me and went into the parlor. So he could have the last word, I reckon.

But he should of knowed it would just make me worse. For after that I wasn't really thinkin about Randall at all. I was thinkin about how I had to show up Daddy and make my own choices and still come out ahead.

Well, to make a long story short, we were married two weeks after that. I'm not sure Randall ever knew what was happenin to him, for I had really poured it on in that time, and we never even paid any thought to where we was to live or how. For we'd just rented us a little coal camp shack with next to nothin in it when all of a sudden, after about three days, we realized that, even if he could make enough to make up that month's rent, we'd *still* not have enough to buy any furniture.

Before that, it was almost like bein at a party, what with bein newlyweds and all. We were havin a good time just ridin up and down those old mountain highways where ever few miles you'd see a sign that said Prepare to Meet Your God, like maybe he was some old man hitch-hikin around the next bend, or there'd be a sign would say Ye Must Be Born Again. But then after that third day, he was out doin some kind of fixup job and I was determined to begin the work of bein a wife, and I saw there wasn't nothin to clean or wash, and not but a little bit to cook.

Well I fixed up what little we had and I just sat on the porch then, thinkin and bitin my nails. And finally he pulled up. He didn't even stop to talk. "Start packin up," he said. And he walked right on past me into the house.

I hollered, "What did you say?"

And he come back out of the house with his guitar case in his hand. "Pack up," he said. And he threw the guitar into the back seat of the car and drove off.

Well I was in a kind of shock for a minute. He hadn't ever spoke to me like that before, you see. Always before, he was cuttin up most of the time. Not that he was ever a clown, and he could go for an hour, if he was in a gang of people, and never say a word. But when he spoke, he'd almost always make some sort of joke. Unless it was a fight. Then he didn't waste no words at all. He said what he had to say and he got down to it.

But this was the first time he had ever spoke like that to me or bossed me and I thought, "Well I guess this is what bein married is all about." But somethin in me pulled away from that, and I was thinkin that's just awful. And I came real close to just settin there on that porch til he'd come back and then I'd tell him he'd have to tell me what this was all about before I turned a hand.

But then I thought, if I don't pack, and he goes wherever he's goin without me, I never will find out what this is all about. Whatever it is, it'll be somethin new. It won't be the same old thing. And besides, I thought, if I don't pack, and we have a big fight over this and he goes off without me, I knew, I just knew, that there would be Daddy just grinnin at me like a possum suckin on an egg.

So I packed. It wasn't much of a job, just a few clothes and some things to cook in.

When he come back, he didn't have the guitar no more. And I didn't ask. You could see he wasn't in no mood. We loaded up the car and got in and he started it up and we drove all that night til we got to the city.

2.

When she first felt the baby move she was in her chair at the window watching the play of lights on the street and the sad work of the women on the corner, the women she still could not believe were prostitutes no matter how much he teased her about being green.

But how could they be? When they leaned into a window of a car they always looked hard enough, and shifty as horsetraders. She could tell they were probably wheeling and dealing and settling on a place to go or settling on whatever it was people had to settle in such a deal. But when they went back against the wall, each of them looked scared, frail as grass. Worry slanted across each face like the rain in November.

Each time a car slowed down at the corner, the girl would hide that fear and worry as she smiled to the curb.

How hungry would a woman have to get, she wondered, before she would have to go down to the corner like that and bargain with some man who was a stranger and who wanted her for things that she could not do yet for the man she had married. Was it hunger at all? Or some other kind of hunger? The women of the corner were strangers to her, sad, defeated, totally unknowable.

It had just turned dark, on a Friday night, and she had no idea if he would be home on time, or if he would work overtime, or if he were spending his brief check.

She watched one of the women, a girl really, her hands in the pocket of her vinyl jacket. The girl's eye followed a car around the corner. Her gaze pivoted like the hand of a clock.

A sudden angry thought rushed through her: What if he's usin them damn (there I'm cussin again) whores?

The thought angered her so that she could no longer sit. She stood and crossed the room.

That son of a (I got to quit this cussin).... Where is he?

The simmering beans on the stove called her and she checked

them, added water to them, and held the lid, thinking, Here I am stuck in this apartment boilin these (quit cussin) beans and readin True Confessions and he's likely out there somewhere (don't say it) with a whore—I mean, prostitute, doin whatever the—whatever it is they do. On our money. Flat broke, rent to pay. Just barely paid off the bill at the store.

She threw the spoon into the churning beans. "Hell with him." And the hell with his beans.

She clamped the lid back down on them as she felt the anger drain out of her. What rose up instead was a wall of loneliness around her: the apartment, the city, the traffic sounds that never, never stopped. The voices in the walls that spoke in anger, laughter, drunkenness, or love, and that never, never had a word for her. The lights from the streets, the music that drifted upward from the bars. The streetvoices of old men and children and winos. She was locked away from it all by fear, by pride.

I reckon it's my own fault, she thought. I just sit here, half afraid, half waitin to be asked.

She went back to the window thinking she would watch again the women of the corner. But even before she could search them out on their patrols, she felt a throb in the lower part of her belly. Then another throb. Then a kick with such force that she eased herself into the chair.

Oh my God, she thought. It really is in there.

She sat in her windowchair with her hands on her belly, wondering how something so small could make a thump so big, wondering what it might be learning as it tumbled, wondering whether her anger had been translated to it.

Sometimes it seemed to sleep. Then it would kick again.

She was not sure how long she sat there before he came in. She just knew, a moment before he spoke, that he was behind her.

"Whassamatter wyou?" he said.

She thought, I reckon I do look sort of foolish, even to a drunk man. She looked up. He was sweating. His eyes were swelled like he'd lost sleep or taken a beating. He was swaying slightly, leaning forward until he lost his balance, then rocking back on his heels and leaning forward again.

"Don't yknow yer beans rgonna burn?" he asked.

For a moment she was scared. She had never seen him this drunk before. He's never yet hit me before, she thought, nor even started to, but I never yet seen him this drunk before. She studied his face, but saw no sign she recognized.

"Don't yknow..."

"The baby's movin," she said, almost in self-defense.

"What?"

"The baby's movin inside of me."

He stared at her. His mouth began to purse around the question again.

"The baby," she said, angry this time, thinking, He's got no business gettin this drunk if he can't understand simple talkin. "It's movin. Inside of me."

"What's it doin?"

"I can feel it kickin inside of me. Ever couple seconds, I can feel it go kathump."

"Kickin you?"

"Or else buttin me with its head, one."

"When...?"

"Just a little bit ago, just before you stumbled in. Ow."

"Whassat?"

"It done it again."

"Well goddam." He stood up, rubbing his eyes, his face, and the back of his neck. Then he raised his hand. "Wait just a little bit," he said, turning back toward the door.

"Where you goin?"

He turned back toward her again. "Wait just a couple minutes."

"Where the hell" (Quit cussin) "Where the.... Where you goin?"

He had gone. She heard his footsteps down the stairs.

She stood up and walked into the kitchen to see the open door empty onto the grey and soundless stairway. She shook with anger and shook shook with the tumbling of the fetus. The beans gave a hint of a smell of burn, so still shaking, she turned to cut off the flame under the pot. Then, as anger suddenly washed over her, she jerked the spoon out of the hot beans and flung it out the door. It hit against the hallway wall, skittered across the bannister, and rang down the steps to the landing.

The sound rang for seconds in her ear. She heard a neighbor door open and she could almost see the curious ear that had wondered at the stairway noise. My lord, she thought, what'll them people think now? She knew that the hidden ears must have by now a catalogue of their noises: his steps, her tears, the shatter of

32

glass, I'm-getting-on-the-next-bus-out-of-here and Well-by-God-I'm-gonna-buy-you-the-ticket, the sounds they made with their bed, the alarm clock's ring, the clanging alarm clock thrown against a wall, her nightmare scream, his songs drunk or sober, her floorwalking and cursing.

Now this, she thought, and for a moment she even believed they could hear the thumping of the child that she heard through her own blood and over the sobs and the curses that she fed to the walls and windows of her room.

Later, after she had done with waiting and had gone to bed, she heard out of the hollow of her sleep, his voice, the sound of snaps like a suitcase and a hollow, wooden bumping noise.

"Hey girl," he said.

No, she thought, no. She stayed in the dark ground of her sleep.

"Hey girl. Listen to this." The first chord was wrong. "Wait." She could hear the string stretch as he retuned. "There." The chord was true.

"What did you go and do?"

He said nothing. He said nothing for the next hour as he played one tune after another, never looking her in the eye but always looking to where her belly swelled the blanket, and somehow, keeping time with the thumping of the child within her. She listened in amazement, gratitude, fear.

III

1.

I can't play somethin I don't believe in. There was this boy that
wanted me to play "Milk Cow Blues" and a bunch of old stuff with
him. He said, "You learn that and we'll have a show." Or else you
get people wantin to hear somethin like "Yellow Ribbons" or
somethin full of flats and minors. They can't just play a straight
Bluegrass song where you can just get down on those strings and
tell it like it is. They got to throw in all those flats and minors and
silly stuff to throw you off the track.

In a good Bluegrass song, you got just three straight chords.
Sometimes you might have an odd one, like "Down in the Willow
Garden" has a minor and "Milwaukee" has an extra chord thrown
in just to make a little different sound. But in a good Bluegrass
song anybody can find the chord and get right in. As long as you
know your chords and the pick and strum, you can play right
behind Bill Monroe himself.

But when they throw in all those minors and odd chords, that's
just to throw you off, keep the music out of reach.

That's why country music today is the way it is. Years ago, you
take Jimmie Rodgers or Hank Williams, or the Carter Family, or
Bill Monroe, any of them, any poor man—or woman either one—
could get em a guitar and a song or two and make it. Course,
there's a lot that never did, but there was always the chance.

But now, there's not that chance. You look at the country music
big shots today, they're not comin off no farms.

Just like the man says, "The workin man can't get nowhere
today."

The real country music isn't in Nashville anymore. There aint
nobody really into country that can write a song about their vaca-
tion in Jamaica or takin the early flight to Florida. Country music
is about dirt on your hands or losin your woman or gettin throwed
in jail or gettin drunk or walkin the floor.

Them people running Nashville now, they aint had no dirt on
their hands. They're just coastin on what the others built for em.

But when somethin really new comes up again, it'll not be out of
Nashville. It'll be out of these little bars, or some road house, or

34

somebody's kitchen. Cause that's where it all comes from, where people really live.

2.

Music in the kitchen: a Perry County fiddler with his hair done golden over grey and his velvet jacket, that hippie kid that played the mandolin, a cousin from the country who had just learned the chorus and the pick and strum. Fire on the Mountain, roll in my sweet, foggy mountain break it down, note by note: Randall's hand swept up the guitar neck to the spot he knew was right. That boy on the rhythm guitar was nailing it down like a carpenter. He worked his way back down the trellis of frets in six-note flurries, all the way back down to the Low E in the minor, up into the center note in the chord, then back into the full chord. As he ended the lick, he felt everyone in the room rock back in admiration, just before the fiddler hit it again.

3.

Friday night crowded, bar maids moving through the tables, the blue and red piping of the neon in the windows, the amber glow of the bottles back of the bar: they were ready. He looked to the fiddler and a tough grass of melody grew out into the crowd, and all ears turned to the stage as the banjo, mandolin, guitar and bass chorded all at once and picked through the first round.

> *Good mornin, Captain!*
> *Good mornin, bo-hoy!*
> *Do you need another muleskinner*
> *Out on your new mud line?*

Shouts, laughter, a wave of talk that rose higher than before the song.

> *Roll in my sweet baby's*

Hands clapping. A beer bottle tilts. Woman alone in the corner, watching the stage, her cigarette tilting like a flag.

> *Lay around the shack till*

Her man came back to the booth. They talked, and the eyes of both went to the stage.

> *I know your parents don't like me.*

The fallen beer bottle rolls to the table edge. Caught by a barmaid. Without stopping, she crosses to the bar and shouts an order.

> *Roll in my sweet baby's arms.*

One final slap on the bass. Shouts

"We thank you. We'll try and do requests when we can—Buddy, I don't know that one."

Slow one:

> *Some people drink champagne*
>   *out under the stars,*
> *While others drink wine,*
>   *leaning over the bar.*

Pick it up again.

> *Well, I'll pawn you my gold watch*
>   *and chain, love,*
> *and I'll pawn you my gold wedding ring*
> *and I'll pawn you this heart*

Keep the harmony sharp as the head of an axe.

> *only say that you love me again.*

Warm beer to ease the throat. Fingers loose. Let that fiddler work awhile: Salt Creek. Sally Goodin. A sound tough as fescue. The banjo laying down a hard rain of notes. Dancers, eight or ten moving shuffle-footed, wide-armed, easily as birds. One woman glanced a grinning glance to him, then looked away. The mandolin shot small sparks in among their feet.

The dancers went back to their seats. Where did that one go? Jimmy Brown, good song for flat picking. Make it ring like a bell.

I wonder how the old folks are at home
I wonder

Now where did she get to? The quick work of the barmaids. Five quick beers at the foot of the stage. Somebody bought a round for the boys in the band.

Yes, I wonder how

4.

Thumpastringringing:
into his sleep:
a thump and an unchorded ringing of wood and steel. He knew that thinringing steel, that wooden thump behind it, and a reflex anger rose up like a broad-winged owl into his sleep.

Every time!

There was never a day when he was not interrupted out of that blazing daylong sleep that followed his third-shift night's work. Not even the blanket pinned across the window could calm that sleep because from around the hem of the blanket, a small white ferret of light hunted in the room, insisting itself into his sleep.

Each day, his sleep was filled with sounds no one should have to sleep with: the games and arguments of the boys, visitors come to gossip, the landlord, the phone, the television, the phones and

37

televisions of the neighbor apartments, a game of ball out in the street, the radio turned up loud for somebody's favorite song. All these would press on him so that even in his sleep he would join in the argument, joke, or song and the pressing sounds and that hunter of light would finally wake him. Grumbling, drunk with daylight and exhaustion, he would join her for coffee and gossip.

Stringringing: the sound that bothered his sleep.

Stringringing: the sound of the six unfingered strings, hand-strummed: that was the name of that sound, he knew. Now who? The kids.

He turned with the wide wing of his anger to where he knew the guitar case to be, to where he knew the boy had stolen in, had pulled out the case, silently unsnapped the latches, then sat down with the guitar on the couch opposite, bumped it against the arm of the couch, then strummed, strummed, strummed.

Why don't she teach them to leave things alone?

That he had not one untampered possession or one uninterrupted hour. That his sleep was lit up with an electrical piping like the neon in a bar window. That these kids, hungry as mice, devoured every minute. His muttering had stopped the strumming. His eyes were open now and he saw the boy on the couch, head, knees and arms: the wide box of the guitar propped in front of him, his left hand stretched out with the neck, his right hand hanging across the front, his fingers barely touching the strings. The forehead tuft of the boy's hair was ruffled like the headfeathers of a small forest bird. The boy's eyes were guiltless, but he was crouching slightly, as if he thought he should hide behind the body of the guitar. He was waiting to see what his father would do.

The sight of the boy shook him, almost like a memory. The boy was too small for this anger.

He turned, pulled the blanket over his head, and dove, like an owl, into the darkest corner of his sleep.

5.

—These cops look tough, but they aint nothin. There was one time I whipped three of em—or nearly whipped em. My car got hit in Covington by a good-lookin woman. Just smacked me right in the back end, and I figured we'd just wait for these police, and let her buy me a new car. Well, by and by this cop came along and he pulls her aside to write it up and pretty soon she's smilin at him and he's smilin at her and he calls me over and asks me some questions and the upshot of it is, I get a ticket. Well, I said, you monkey-suited son of a bitch. Then he grabbed me by the shirt and right away I hit him. Well, I don't even know where they came from, but the next thing I knew they had me. It took three of em though. They handcuffed me and put me in a car and took turns beatin me all the way out to Latonia and back. And I was fightin em the whole time, handcuffs and all. And I must have been fightin em pretty good, cause finally they took me back to town and put me in front of a judge. And that judge, he was sidin with them, but still he said, "It took three of you? Why you look worse that he does." For three days nobody knew where I was or nothin. I couldn't make a phone call, send a message or nothin.

—And when I'd call, they wouldn't tell me nothin.

—I kept askin guys that were gettin out to take her a message, but they never did. Til finally one guy—

—It was a cab driver.

—He was gettin out so I told him about it and he promised to tell her where I was.

—And he did.

—So she started comin to see me.

—But you couldn't really see him. Poor Randy, he was just a baby then, he'd just cry. Course he could hear him and know it was him, but you couldn't really see him on account it was this wire mesh over the window.

—It was about four days after that they finally let me out. She talked that judge into it.

—I think he finally got tired of seein me. I'd be there ever mornin first thing tryin to get him out on bond. And then he let him go.

—I think whippin those cops helped too, cause at the trial they didn't talk no more about it takin three of em. They wouldn't of been able to hold their heads up. So I did some days for it. But I promised myself I'd get even with that first cop. And I did. I got him right in front of my house. I looked out the window and I seen him settin there in his car. So I went out, walked around the block, came up on him, jerked him out of that car and had him out cold before he knew who hit him.

—And all he did to Randall was tear the buttons off his shirt.

—He was just laying there on the street.

—I was afraid he'd killed him. He came runnin in the house, all proud, sayin Mommy, Mommy, look what I done.

—Then I stood there lookin out the window lookin at em lookin after me.

—I was afraid they'd come up there though and find him.

—That would of been one dead cop. I had a .38 in my hand. He'd of been dead soon as he walked in that door.

—But they just looked and hunted and never did find anything.

—And if any of the neighbors ever saw, they never said a word.

6.

We seen some hard times through the years. There was times he'd have to sell the guitar just to get food for the babies. He'd hock it out and he might get it back or he might not. And if he didn't, well, he'd get him another hock shop guitar til the next time he'd get laid off or fired or disgusted.

We had cars that you wouldn't believe. There was one old Mustang that wouldn't start unless you pushed it, just two or three feet, but that's what it would take. There was another that didn't have no reverse so you never could park anyplace you had to back out of. And there was another that didn't have no brakes, but we took it from Fort Wayne, Indiana, to Hazard, Kentucky, anyway. When we got there he got set to get his tools out. I said, "Why bother now?"

We've lived in Fort Wayne, Louisville, Covington, Mount Vernon, Kentucky, Hazard, Cincinnati, and a hundred different apartments. We might live in three different apartments in three months. Sometimes we moved from evictions. Sometimes so we could skip a rent. Sometimes it was for the rats or for the neighbors or else just for the dark stairways.

Sometimes we'd move together, but a couple times, I'd just up and move on my own. He'd be gone, you see, and he'd stay gone for a week or two. He might be shackin up somewhere or he might be layin up drunk at some buddy's house. He might of took off lookin for a job or somebody give him a job drivin a truck to someplace halfway across the country. It might be any one of them things, I never did get the low-down on all the things he done, but I heard enough stories to fill a book.

Well, anyway, I'd say the heck with this. If I'm gonna be livin by myself, I might as well be livin where I want to live. So I'd find me a job and I'd pull out.

I mainly worked waitress jobs. Sometimes it might be some kind of factory or a warehouse, but mostly it was bein a waitress. Those are the easiest to get, and a woman out on her own has got to get somethin quick.

Bein a waitress don't look hard, waitin on tables or workin a counter, but it's work, just like anything else. You're on your feet the whole time, tryin to keep track of orders and the money, and you've got to work over that hot grill scrapin that grease and flippin those eggs. And you've got to make that coffee and keep an eye out that no customers walk out without payin or there aint no drunks fallin asleep in the back booth and you've got to flip that hamburger before it burns. I swear, it'll make your head spin. I'd get so tired at the end of the day I could just barely walk home. And then there'd be the babysitter to pay off and the kids to take care of.

Well, he'd solve that for me. Ever time I'd get me a job, he'd make sure I lost it. He'd find out where I was workin and he'd begin callin the boss or makin some kind of trouble til, sure enough I'd get fired. There was one time he come right in the restaurant and just sat there in front of a cold cup of coffee for two hours til I got so nervous I smashed a whole stack of plates right there on the floor right in front of him. Well, he just grinned and walked out.

41

So we seen some hard times through the years. Not so much the early years. He seemed like he was tryin to prove himself then, and whatever job he took, he'd stick it out long as he could. He just couldn't take ahold of anything that would last. Either he'd get laid off or he'd get fired over some little bit of nothin. Or else some foreman would begin to workin on him til he couldn't take it no more. But after the third and the fourth, he begun to get more nervous—like, more hard to predict. And he might walk off any old job. And he might disappear any old time.

Not that he'd ever stop carin. How can I explain it? I don't really understand it myself, cause even though he put us through a lot of trouble and hardship, it wasn't that he didn't care. It's just that, with the way he was raised, and the way the times were, he couldn't keep it all together. He couldn't be a rounder and a family man both, but he wanted to do both. You knew he loved the bars and the honky tonks. And you knew he wanted for his kids what he'd missed as a child. And these were a kind of war inside of him. He couldn't have it both ways, and he knew it. And as the years went on, it pressed on him more and more. And he seemed like he knew those heart attacks were comin. Or that somethin was comin, and he didn't know what.

So I couldn't bring myself to hold it against him or to break up with him or to hate him, even when I wanted to kill him.

IV

1.

He felt it first as a narrow worm of pain worrying beneath his breastbone. It grew slowly until it woke him out of a fearful sleep and he lay in the warmth of his blankets, afraid to breathe for fear of disturbing what had grown into a cramped and heated serpent.

He had not yet tried to move. The muscles of his temples tightened against the thought that his legs, his arms had lost themselves in the grasses, that he could move nothing but his flickering eyes.

He looked to the dresser top where the clock was ticking softly as a cricket. He could see the greenish glow of the hands and the numbers, but no matter how he squinted he could not make out the time. There was no other sound but the breathing of his wife and the breathing of his children. There was nothing alight but the glowing, fragmented eye of the clock.

Finally, he dared a breath, and as he slowly swelled his chest, he felt the tunnel that held the pain press like a mole heap against the heavy stone of his breast. He felt the blind pain stir and push against the walls of his chest and strain against the trap of his ribs.

He let out the breath, but the swollen pain did not subside. Angry, blind, trapped, the pain had wakened full now and spread across his chest, stiffening its muscle and sharpening its nerve.

Will it go away? Maybe it'll go away. The thought did not stop the hardening of his temples nor the scattered running of his fears.

He peered once again toward the clock, thinking, *The alarm'll go off sometime soon.*

He thought about trying to move, but decided against it. He lay still as a rabbit under the green glowing eye of the clock and the hunter's hidden eye of his pain.

At least, he thought, *I got a good excuse for skippin work.*

•　　•　　•

The clanging alarm broke into her sleep like a mugger, and she lay, as always, waiting for him to answer it. But as always, it continued to clang at her, and as always, she threw back the blankets to shut it off.

Why in the world can't he get that alarm hisself? she thought.

She pitched forward out of the bed, stumbling over his shoes, cursing silently, and reaching out for the clock. She missed once, then found it. Her eyes were not yet focused, her balance not yet steady. "It's time to get up," she said, yawning so wide she had to steady herself against the dresser.

Most days, once she had spoken, she would hear him roll over and moan. This day, when she heard nothing, she thought, *It'll be a hard time gettin him up today.* She remembered that he had come in late and tired with his guitar after she had already gone to bed. When she turned in her sleep to greet him she remembered his silence and the strange worried look on his face and that he sat down slowly at the edge of the bed, that he lay back slowly and buried his face into the pillow.

Now, as she turned from the clock to cross back to his side of the bed, she was thinking of how she would have to push at him and shake him until he began to shake his head, curse, and rise up out of his sleep.

But he was already sitting up against the headboard. *My God*, she thought, *is he dead?* His eyes were open. He was staring at his knees. Both hands were pressing on his chest.

She stood at the bedside for a moment, trying hard to think, but no clear thought came to her. Finally, she knew, *I've got to check him. I've got to see what it is.*

She remembered: Hold a mirror to a dying person's mouth: If the white rose of that person's breath formed on the mirror, then that person was still alive. She wanted to try that before she moved him or touched him, for the white arms of her fear moved along her shoulders. *What if he's dead?*

She breathed deeply. *Then he's just dead*, she thought. *One way or another, I got to find out.*

She crouched at the bedside and looked up into his face. The blue-grey light from the window was framing him. A muscle on his cheek was pulsing slightly, bringing his cheek in and out of shadow. His eyes were on her, weak as prayer.

"What is it?" she asked him.
"Babe," he whispered. "It hurts. It hurts real bad."
"What hurts?"

He moved his hand across his chest. "Right...through...here."

She got up and switched on a light, then bent down to examine his bare chest.

"I can't see nothin."

He shook his head slowly. "I can't hardly breathe," he said.

"Did you hurt yourself last night?"

"If I did," he whispered, "I was too drunk to feel it right then."

"What are we gonna do?"

"I don't know." Then he raised an eyebrow. "Maybe I need to get drunk again."

●　　　●　　　●

Within the next two hours, she had hustled the older boys off to school, called his job, and helped him to the armchair in the living room. Propped up with a pillow, he could breathe more easily and the pain shifted some of its weight from his chest.

"Don't you reckon we ought to go to the hospital?"

He said nothing.

"You don't have to drive. I can call the life squad."

"I'll be gone out that door before they ever get here."

"Do you know what it is that's wrong with you?"

"My chest hurts."

"Well, what kind of hurt is it?"

"Goddam it, woman. It just hurts."

●　　　●　　　●

By the third day, I knew he was too weak to do anything about it, so I went ahead and called the life squad. He could just barely move to go to the bathroom. He didn't even try to go to the table to eat, and what he ate was just a bite or two at a time. He couldn't breathe if he laid down, so of a night I had to prop him up with pillows in the chair and that's where he slept.

When the life squad come in, he looked over at me and cussed a couple times and he made like he was gonna fight em, but after a minute or two he looked sort of relieved. He didn't try to fight.

You see, he was afraid of goin to the hospital, cause he can't stand to be tied down. But after awhile, that pain scared him more. He didn't know anything about a heart attack or what kind of chance he had or what he'd have to face in the hospital, but I think

45

he was afraid that, whatever it was, it was awful bad, and he'd have to lay up for months, and that maybe he'd never be well again. He was more afraid of that than he was of dyin.

And I think he was afraid of how he'd not be his own boss once the doctors got hold of him. And that's why he hoped it would go away and he could nurse himself through it, to prove he could, even with all that pain.

Of course, you don't know. You can't really know with someone like him.

So he went into the hospital, and I had the job then of earnin a livin. I went down to the welfare for some help, but it's just like havin a full-time job, what with all the papers and waitin in line and meetin with caseworkers and buyin your food stamps and everbody breathin down your neck, and I figured, for all this trouble I might as well be workin.

Well, I didn't know how much trouble there was. Cause like I've said before, about all I could go into was waitressin, and with that you've got to get your uniform and hustle all them orders and deal with all the men, you know, makin passes, and hope they'll leave some kind of a tip cause they don't pay hardly nothin. And the jobs don't last anyway. The main problem is a babysitter. Especially if you don't have family nearby. So you leave em with a neighbor or some friend or even with a stranger that you hire. It'll go all right til the first time one of em gets sick or the babysitter quits on you and you're late for work or else you don't make it in. They'll drop you real quick and take on somebody else, and there's nothin you can do cause there's nobody in a little place like that that can speak up for you. You've got no rights, and they can do whatever they want.

But even if they want to treat you right, they can't hardly. Some of these little places, they're just barely makin a go of it themselves, workin fourteen or fifteen hours a day, and you might be takin home as much as they are.

So anyway, that's how we had to live after that, cause Randall, he just went from hospital to hospital after that, while they tested him and worked on him. And finally they decided it was a bad valve in his heart and it was backin up blood in his heart and smotherin him. And they figure it was from the rheumatic fever he'd had as a child.

And that's when they begun to load him up on pills. He'd be bleary-eyed and his tongue would get all thick like a shag carpet. They tinkered around with him for awhile—a little bit more of this, a little bit less of that—til they thought they got it right. But still, it changed him.

I can't say for sure how it changed him. There was a different look to his eyes. There was a nervous look about him. He always seemed to be lookin back over his shoulder. And this is the hard part—he always seemed like he was afraid of someone sneakin up on him. Not another person, not a real person. But it was like, right behind his shoulder, there was somebody comin up from behind him. It was awful, watchin him. I don't know what he was afraid of most—the hospitals, or dyin, or the thought that he couldn't do like he wanted no more.

Then finally they sent him to Alabama where they did the open heart surgery.

2.

It was the first thing that he heard as he came out of the anasthetic haze: The distant sound of a man with a hammer. A sound from within a fog. A mile away, a man labored with a hammer at a spike. He took neither rest nor pause, never missed, never jogged out of rhythm, never skipped a beat.

The hammer drilled in time with the dull pain of the needle in his arm, with the slow drum in his ears, with the throb in the bones above his eyes.

He opened his eyes and looked down to his arm and, though it hurt his eyes and head to do it, followed the tube that trailed out his wrist up to a bottle on a stand.

Hospital, he thought. *I reckon I lived through it.*

47

He looked around the room to see what gadget was making the sound, and twisting around, stretched his sutures. The new pain burned across his chest and he settled back against the pillow. But he had seen the green glow of the monitor at his head. *That's it,* he thought. Satisfied, he drifted back to sleep with the green glow still in his eye and the trick of the hammer striking his ear.

Later, the doctor told him what it was.

"It's what?"

"It's the valve we installed. You hear it with each heartbeat. The valve allows blood to flow from one chamber into another so that it can be pumped through your lungs. That's what was wrong with you before. Your heart had been scarred, perhaps by a childhood fever, the blood was backing up in one chamber, and oxygen was not reaching your blood. That's why you couldn't catch your breath. The mechanical valve allows...."

"I know all that, goddammit. But what's that noise."

"That's the valve."

"What do you mean it's the valve?"

"You can hear the piston click back into place each time your heart pumps."

"And how long is that gonna go on?"

"Well, obviously, as long as your heart keeps beating."

When he leaped for the doctor, the monitor stopped, the IV tube jerked out of his arm, and four of his stitches broke. And though he laid for another day with his arms strapped at his sides with tranquilizers filling his skull with cloud and a patrol of interns and psychologists, he was happy to know, after an orderly told him, that he had broken the jaw of the doctor.

3.

She heard the new sound in the silence after a dark and drumming rain. He had come back from the Birmingham hospital in a hard silver dusk, an early winter rainstorm. The rain pattered across the hood of the cab that had brought him home. It obscured his face behind the cab's blind windows. It beat against the kitchen windows and rattled against their words as the boys opened their presents and as they shared their first coffee. It spattered through the hours until sometime in the late night hours the silence and the new sound woke her.

What time is it? She looked for the clock. In the dim blue street-. light from the window, the dark hands told her it was half past three.

Click
Click
Click

Clear as the ticking of a clock. Slow as breath. It had not startled her. She felt as if the sound had been there all along. As she listened, she heard other sounds that had been there all along. The hiss of the space heater as it burned. The tousling of the boys in their blankets. The low hum of the electric clock. The tiny creaks of the furniture as each piece settled further into place. The low shudder of brick and joist settling more comfortably into each other, and the stones of the foundation settling down into the earth.

But each of these were sounds that she knew, sounds to which she could give a name.

This sound was slower than the ticking of a clock. But just as sure. Steady as breath or blood.

She looked around her and saw no sign. She looked over the dresser and its knickknack army, the sentinel bedposts, the yellow glow of the heater, the tumble of bedclothes, his sleeping chest that slowly rose and fell.

She looked again at the scar that split his chest. A straight narrow line, it lay across him dark as a leech.

49

Click
Click
Soon, the sound itself became one of the sounds that she knew.
Click
Click
Clean as the ticking of a clock. Steady as blood or breath.
And she slept.

4.

—She told me, after that heart attack, that was a sign I ought to slow down.

—He should, really. Out all night in some bar playing music. Never eatin right. Missin your pills. Doin who-knows-what-else. You should slow down.

—Look, when you...

—And them friends of yours don't care.

—...when you...

—They'll let you run yourself to death, and me and these boys'll be...

—Look, I said, when you see me...

—...me and these boys'll be left on our own and them friends...

—When you see me slowin down...

—....These so-called friends of yours, these drinkin buddies of yours aint gonna take up for us.

—When you see me slowin down, it'll be for the last stop.

V

Oh can't you see that distant train
Come whirling around the bend.
It's taking away my own true love
To never return again.

All the good times are past and gone
All the good times are gone.
All the good times are past and gone.
Darling don't you weep for me.

1.

Trick

Trick

Trick
Just waitin it out.

Trick
That's all I'm a doin. Just

Trick
waitin it out. Pretty soon,
Trick
it'll get me.
Gotta do my time,
Trick
Gotta do my time.
With an achin heart
Trick
And a worried mind.

All this bother aint solved a thing.

    Trick
It just put off what was gonna
come
    Trick
 anyway. It's what nobody
can put off forever.
    Trick
    I haven't bought a thing worth
havin
    Trick
    with it.
    I'd rather be in some dark hollow
    Trick
    Where the sun don't ever shine
    Than to be in some big city
    Trick
    In a small room with trouble on my mind
    So why
        did I let them
    Trick
    trick me?

2.

The worst part, I think, was after he found out he wouldn't be
able to work again, but they wasn't gonna give him his pension
either. They said he could work, you see, but he couldn't do
manual labor, that's all. But that's the only labor he'd ever done.
Except for music, but that was only nickel and dime stuff. A man
can't make a real livin for a family that way, not unless he makes
the big time, and that's only the very few.

So that meant he wouldn't be able to work, but by *sayin* he was
able to work, that cut him out of the pension. People told him he

ought to get a lawyer and fight it, but he wouldn't. He wouldn't do that because he felt like they owed it to him, and if they wasn't gonna give it up, then he wasn't gonna beg. I would of fought em, but that wasn't his way of fightin.

So anyway, that meant the only way we could live was by welfare or by me workin, which suited me fine. I like workin and makin ' my own money, even if it's only a little bit. So I went back to workin, mainly through temporary labor, here and there, whenever I could. And he went back to wreckin my jobs, one after another, until after the third one or so, he just quit. I don't know why, but it seemed like he'd accepted it, that the only way we was to live was if I worked. But he still had a hard time of it.

3.

Sixteen pills a day, the bottles arranged in rank along the dressertop. Beer-bottle-brown plastic with white press-down-twist-off caps, and the typed-in white labels. A chart taped to the wall showing when to take each one, morning, noon, and night. Gelatin caps full of beads or dust: red, yellow, white, and blue. Buff-colored buttons. Tablets shaped like miniature coffins. Water pills. Pills to thin the blood. Pills against the chance of infection. Pills for the clock-like regulation of the beat of his heart. Pills to undo the effects of the pills and to drive a sharp nail of light through the fog raised by the others.

There were days when that nail was a spike of pain down the middle of his skull and he would walk from bar to restaurant to bar and back to keep from holding still and to try to dull the edge of that pain with beer, talk, motion until the shortness of his breath left him wheezing against a wall hearing his blood thunder in his ear and the tiny iron valve ticking with it in his chest.

There were days when he stayed behind the fog like an iceberg, sitting in his kitchen chair behind a cup of coffee, mute, his eyes like two resting sea birds.

Days when he sat behind those blackbird eyes at the windows of the Red Barn restaurant with his hands around cold coffee in a paper cup and watched: the red faces of the winos bumming change, passing a bottle around. Children whose armloads of books slipped away from them onto the sidewalk or who ran and shouted with their free hands raised. The young girls who looked as if they lived on twinkies and hard drugs. Old people who walked with crutches, canes, walkers, who walked slowly, who walked not at all but rolled by on wheelchairs or who walked awhile then stood awhile or who looked down at the others from upstairs windows. A Black man with a shaved head and both fists clenched. Newsboys with their lumpy bags across their shoulders. Men with black lunchpails, women in white waitress uniforms. The women in hairnets and green dresses who worked in the laundry.

Days when he never left the house for the pain or for the stiffness of his left arm or for the massive work of breathing or for that fog which no sun would lift.

Days when he drank until he could forget who he was or where he belonged and he stayed drunk enough to end up on someone's couch or some new woman's bed. When he stayed away out of shame or fear until the pills ceased to work and fear camped in his belly. When finally he returned, too fearful even to feel shame.

Days when he held his cup of coffee in the kitchen and watched the boys play and argue and smudge their schoolwork and grow.

Days when he tried to pick at the guitar, when he tried to move the numb fingers of his left hand into their places on the neck.

Days when all he heard was the ugly ticking in his breast.

Days when he looked at her, at the children, at his own softened hands and felt a strange battle take place behind his eyes.

Enough of days.

4.

The pills: he must have swallowed a fistful, she thought. The plastic brown bottle was crushed and splintered on the dressertop.

They were the...whatchamacallems: the two-a-day pills. One of them had escaped and rolled up against the nail clippers. Another was crushed to white powder among the pocket change.

He was reeling on the edge of the bed, bare-chested and pale, his breast-bone scar bright as the line in a thermometer. His eyes were closed. His brow was flexed and wrinkled. His fists, each of them at his sides, propping him up, were clenched.

What do I do?

"Hey," she shouted in his face. "Hey."

She slapped him. He tried to pull away from her, so she took his head in both hands and rocked it back and forth, shouting, "Hey. Wake up."

He raised his eyebrows slightly as if to open his eyes and opened his mouth as if to speak. He shook his head so slowly that at first she thought it had no meaning and that he was tranced by the pills and whatever they were doing within his blood and nerve.

But he aint just driftin off, she thought. *He's workin at it.*

She stood back.

What do I do? The question this time was ringed with horror. *He's workin at it,* she thought, unable, even with all those pills, even with all the flaws of his heart, to break down all those rebels within the bone and nerve and gland that called on him to live. *And still he's working at it.*

And the horror was washed away by an anger that shook her like a hard wind: *No,* she thought, *he aint gonna do that to me.*

"Hey," she shouted, slapped him cheek to cheek like a mound of dough. "Wake up" *you sorry spineless laydown dyin son of a* thinking:

55

He can't quit on me now after years of hardship and a bedroom full of sons. She slapped him and shouted and called for the oldest boy to call the life squad and while he reeled backwards to avoid her, tried to force a finger into his throat to make him vomit up the pills and, once that didn't work, called to the boys for cold water and called out *why aint the life squad here yet* and over and over shouted *Hey. Wake up. Hey* and over and over thinking *he can't quit on me now.*

5.

Within a shell. A dim and diffuse light, more like a dark than a light, wherein no shape moved. He had no notion that he breathed or that he wanted to breathe. A heavy fluid pressed against his ears. A slow cellular hunger. An amniotic drowning. A sleep that was neither dream nor death nor even oblivion.

Which way? It was a question for which he hungered for no answer.

Kachick

Thin drumsound at the edge of hearing.

Kachick

Tin drumsound rattling inside the
hollows of his ear.

Kachick

What is it?

Kachick

What is it?

Kachick

The bastards. He knew. That rhythmic
disruption.

Kachick

Now, cramping limbs. A compressed
skull. Eyes pressed shut. A heart
that demanded new blood.

Kachick

His chest spasmed.

Kachick
The sudden air split him like a
lance. He was
Kachick
     sucking angry rags of air.
The bastards. Why
Kachick
     did they leave me here
like this? He was
Kachick
     alone, blind, and bound.

Why are these straps on my arms? He
wanted
Kachick
her. He wanted her voice. He wanted
to put his hands around the small heads
of his sons.
Kachick
He knew by now that he was
hoarsely screaming and that maybe he
would
now
Kachick
be heard. If they wanted to hear him
at all.
Kachick
So he tried to still his voice and
to slow his breathing which was coming
now in angry flags,
Kachick
     and
calmed himself to keep from alarming
the nurses,
Kachick
     and to keep from being bothered
with their needles and sedatives,
Kachick
     and to
lay, lonely, hungering for a human touch,
Kachick
and laboring against the straps that bound
him, hands and feet.

57

6.

This time, when Daddy came back, he had no new scars. None, at least, that he could see.

What work of trouble was this stay? There had been the sudden scare, the tension of emergency. Heart attack, that was what Mommy had said. But those other times, they had talked about it. Not a lot, but he remembered how they had talked with each other and with visitors about how the hospital had opened him up like a box and put a clock into his heart.

But this time, he muttered, she whispered, if they talked about it at all. And people came to help, but they couldn't speak of it.

All but once. Just one time, he said to her, madder than spit, "Because I wanted to." He looked around and saw that he was watching, but he had already said it, so he went on. "I'm full of pills and hurtin and I can't work. Would you want to live?"

"You hush," she said.
"I'll talk if I want to talk."
"Hush now," she insisted.
"Them pills didn't do it."
"Will you..."
"I didn't take enough or I didn't take the right ones, but I meant business. They sent a shrink out there to ask me why I did it. I told him..."
"Will you be..."
"I told him, look, you think somebody who wants to kill himself is crazy. But here I am, sick, can't work, medication screwin up my head at all hours..."
"Hush," she said again.
"I'll talk if I want to."
"The kids."

When Daddy looked up in the doorway where he stood, he whirled around for a toy, for anything for his hands, to pretend he had not been listening, to deflect that punishing stare.

Daddy crushed his cigarette in the ash tray and got up for more coffee. He turned in mid-cup, and said, to her and to the boys, "Don't you know, I want to live. And not by halves. I want to live."

7.

There was a note he wanted, a particular patch of tone lost in the net of strings. He worked up and down the guitar neck to find it, hammering out a frame for what he felt, a ladder of chord and bending string on which he could climb up out of his hurting. Sweat studded his brow and made a small pool in the small of his back. He was patient. He searched the strings as a hunter sweeps a field.

He picked away at the shell of note until he got down into the heart of what pained him: it nearly fluttered loose, but he caught it, caught it, and caught it again, then released it like a bird out of a trap as he picked his way back down into the full chord. He tapped one more time into that seam for one more piece of what he wanted, then picked it to a close.

He put his hand to the strings to tamp the last shimmer of sound so he could feel for himself what he had done. He was breathing slow and steady as a grey rain. The song had loosened what had been tied in a stiff knot of anger. What he had now was not a smaller hurt but a cleaner hurt, not spoiled by any bitterness. It was a cleaner hurt, made up of roads, flowers at a funeral, houses with black windows, a wrinkled letter, the tumble of her hair where she slept, regret, the hot smell of a railroad tie, the first scrawled letters and numbers of his sons that were black, bleared, and awkward as new birds.

He was breathing slow and steady as a daylong nightlong rain. In some nearby window, he could hear a radio play some other's song.

8.

He keeps busy now, and he don't get so depressed like he used to. He takes an interest in things. He don't say much, ever, but you can see him watching what's goin on, like he's addin it all up.

And he takes more of an interest in the boys now. Before, he loved em and all, but he always seemed worried with em. And he would leave all the responsibility for raisin em to me. Now, he'll watch the kids while I work, and I know that's hard on him. But afterwards, he'll go out and play music somewhere or he'll have people over to play. And he's even been able to make some money here and there playin.

That's where he still runs into trouble now and then, stayin out late in some bar or somebody's house. I tell him he ought to slow down a little, take care of himself.

You know what he'll do? He'll just look away, maybe drum his fingers on the table, a tune or two, then he'll go off and find him somethin else to do.

•   •   •

And then there was the day he told me he wanted me to sing. Of course, he knew how I used to sing growin up, cause I'd talked about it off and on, not really meanin nothin by it. I'll talk about almost anything. But I never did feel comfortable singin around him, not since the first time I saw him. He was just so good that I felt, you know, like I couldn't equal up. And I'm pretty backward about somethin like that anyway.

So except for hummin around or singin a little in my housework, I hadn't really sung in years. Words, I would keep in mind real easy, and like I say, I'd sing a little around the house, but as to really sing, to sing around people, I hadn't done that in years, and never felt I could. Not even when I was young did I ever feel like I was free to sing in front of people, unless it was in church, and that was somethin I didn't want any part of anyway. But that's another story altogether.

60

Anyway, that's how girls was brought up then and that's how I was til one night he had a few friends over to make music. And he says to me, "Sing 'The Knoxville Girl' with me."

Well I reckon I went all red. At least I felt I did, and I got all frustrated and I wanted to leave the room, cause he kept on askin me, "Sing 'The Knoxville Girl' with me," and he knew I knew the words, cause I'd probably hummed it and sung pieces of it a hundred times around the house. But I wasn't ready to sing it out in front of all those people, and each of em good at some kind of music.

Well I begun to think maybe he was drunk, cause he kept at it, but I knew he hadn't had a drop all night. So I don't know what got over him, but he kept pushin at me. Not pushin, really. It was more like he was askin for somethin he wanted real bad. He was almost crying at the end.

So I did it. I can't really tell you what it sounded like, but I can tell you what it felt like. I tried to ignore everybody else in the room and to sing the high part like I did with my sister, and it was like, well, it was like I remember in church with all the singin and preachin and all, there'd be a minute when you'd feel yourself flyin up out of yourself. I'd always hold back on it, cause I felt, and I still do, that it wasn't me, it's just the pull of all those people and of that preacher, and once he's got you up there, he's got you heart and billfold. Well, this was different. It was that same feelin of flyin up out of myself, but it didn't feel like a cheat. It felt right. And once it started, I even thought about singin. I was just hearing two voices, almost like bells ringin, and I just felt so fine and free.

Then it was over, and he put one last lick on his guitar. And wouldn't anybody say a word for a minute, except that hippie kid. He just said "far out," real quiet.

And I looked over at Randall, and he was just grinning like he'd won a bet.

9.

His hands were around another cold cup of coffee at the
restaurant window, watching the flow and counter flow of people.
He came there nearly every day in a spare hour while the boys were
in school and she was at work, on those days when she could get
work. And each day he drank the same cold cup of coffee with the
same pale glaze of cream across the top.

From where he sat:
the sidewalk traffic, those who were selling and those who were
sold, the ones just hanging around and the ones on their way,
a little park where the winos sat on benches like wrecked boats
on a beach,
the front door of a bar, its cold blaze of neon, the chipping red
paint, the black window in the door.

He couldn't remember what he remembered about that bar.

On the sidewalk in front of him, two children played at tetherball. The girl played with a cat-like intensity and the boy could not
keep up. The ball was an empty plastic gallon milkjug, tied to a
signpost by a frayed and patched-together rope. The boy sound-
lessly shouted each time the ball came around to him, but the girl
never spoke. Each time they hit the jug, the sound beat against the
windowpane with an almost visible shimmer, as if a hand had
pressed against the glass.

The boy, who might have been her younger brother, played with
his eye on the ball, following it around the pole and batting at it,
satisfied if he hit it at all and happy at the noise it made. But the
girl watched ahead of the ball. Before she hit it, she had already
judged the arc of the ball, and so she was already watching the boy
to know where she wanted to put it. If he leaned to the left, she had
already judged it and was ready to hit it to his right. Over and
again she frustrated him.

The girl smiled when the boy gave up. She looked around. The
street ignored her small victory. She reached up to take loose the
rope, but it was tied too high. She looked for her brother to boost
him up, but he was already half a block gone.

So she shrugged her shoulders and looked around again. Two of her friends had come up the street on the other side and were leaning against the barwindow. The two friends shouted across to her. Their hands were in their pockets. They chewed gum in a quick rhythm. They each gave a sidelong glance to the man who passed them to enter the bar. *Cocky*, he thought. They shouted to her again, so she left the tetherball hanging from its signpost and stepped out into the traffic.

He would not watch her cross for there were things now he could not watch without a new feeling come over him. He rubbed his forehead to loosen a tightening pain in the bridge of his eyes.

He had seen those girls before, with their friends, had watched them all that winter long with their collars closed around their faces, the winter rain slanting across their faces, and it bothered him that he knew he would see no more what he saw one day from that window: these same girls, with four or five others, in a line, arm in arm, dancing down the long street, the October sun bright on their hair, their jackets, their faces.

The pain above his eyes grew another turn tighter. He closed his eyes and rubbed his forehead until he had unravelled that pain. Then he went home.

10.

City of sleeplessness. The darkness spread out from his window, studded with lights like the tie strings on a quilt: houselights, street lights, stitchery of auto lights, hint of neon.

Unravelling edge of the sheet of streetnoise. Breath-like sound of the lonely buses that glowed in the night like the fish at the bottom of the sea. A shout. Scream of tires. Factory clatter in the graveyard shift. Sounds spread across the city sky. Sounds gathered and woven into one light blanket.

There is never a silence in a city, he knew. Never a time when it stops, when people stop turning engines, strutting the sidewalks, whispering, shouting, laughing, moving trains, making love, shivering, hurting each other, hurting.

A brakeshoe whistled under his window. A wino's wavering song. Distant urgent wheeping of a siren.

A siren always means trouble, he knew. He wondered whose trouble this siren could mean.

He heard her exhausted, job-weary breathing and the restless breathing of the boys.

He could not sleep, and yet he was not restless, as if, this once, he had nothing to fear, as if nothing, even if he let it, nothing could hurt him. Nothing from the present, nor from the future, nor from his shuddering memory:
a thing he had always before muscled back out of mind, a memory that seemed now to him as strangely ordered as dream: Korea: The scarred battlefield where they had sent him: a shattered bamboo house, a crippled fence, the disrupted furrows: a field full of what he thought were corpses.

Yet one moved. Then another: a beckoning arm, a moaning head raised, a voice: *medic*. What he thought was a field of death was instead a field of pain. Those he thought were dead were instead wounded and waiting.

11.

She was waiting at her bus stop in a silvering April mist. It was cold for the season, and a wind pressed the mists against her face. She looked down the long street. The grey head of a bus moved out of the blur of buildings, utility poles, vehicles, and street signs, like a bass stirring in the waters.

She was carrying a heavy dread. *Somethin's gonna happen,* she thought. *Before this day is out.*

The look on his face had told her that as she drank her morning coffee. Across the kitchen table, a grin lit one corner of his face, that little boy look that he had when he was teasing, when he had just gotten away with something, or when he was about to. *He always looks like that when he's gonna pull somethin.* She knew too well: *I know he's gonna pull somethin.*

It had been coming for days. He didn't sleep. He hadn't even come to bed last night. He barely ate. He drank an endless cup of coffee. He lit cigarettes and left them to smoke themselves down as he worked the guitar. Twice, when she got up in the middle of the night, she found him at the kitchen table, working his knuckles into the ridges of his forehead.

And today at the table, that look: *Somethin's gonna happen.* She needed to test him. "Don't forget to get the boys off by eight-twenty," she said.

"Got it," he nodded. The radio was playing. He was humming and tapping his finger on the handle of his cup in a measure slower than the radio's song.

"And Randy needs that note for his teacher."
"Got it covered."
She knew that. He was still humming and tapping in between his words. "It's your pill day, so be sure to get Joey up and get him to the sitter."
"Got it."

The radio tune was over, and the announcer was now trying to sell something, but Randall was still humming and tapping in the same slow measure.

Does he even hear me?

He stopped tapping, reached for his cigarette, and looked up at her.

He knows I'm nervous about somethin and he's playin with me. She said, "Well I'm leavin."

They kissed and she started out, her handbag over her shoulder, her bus change in her fist. At the door, she looked back. His grin was gone. As she left, his finger was slowly tapping on the table-top.

The bus was hers. She could tell it coming from two blocks away.

●   ●   ●

Pill day: He slid down deeper into the black-molded plastic of the chair. He was almost down to his last cigarette. There were still five more people ahead of him.

He knew what would happen. It always happened. The nurse would take his temperature, would take his blood pressure, would ask the same set of questions she always asked. Then as he tried a new set of jokes on her, she would give him the slip to go to the pharmacy.

On this old rockpile

And at the pharmacy, he would wait again: a shorter wait and a different set of chairs, but no different from the time two weeks before or the time two weeks before that

with a ball and chain

nor any different from the time two weeks from now.

They call me by a number
*   not a name*
*   Lord*
*   Lord*

Five more·ahead of him. Twenty more behind him. Some of them he knew. There were jokes, complaints, stories and boasts they had shared as they sat waiting for their names to be called, smoking long chains of cigarettes, reading and wrinkling reams of

66

newspapers, breaking the backs of five hundred Reader's Digests and invoking the ceilings, the walls, and each other's eyes.

Gotta do my time.

They hated it. He hated it. The nurse at the end of the line, in her way, she hated it.

Maybe even the doctors. Maybe even they hated it.

Gotta do my time.

As he looked one way and another down the line and at the orderlies wheeling carts along the aisle, at the patient in his robe working on his crutches toward the end of the hall, at the one-eyed man with his big hands in his lap, at the long-haired kid who was searching his pockets with his hands and searching the ceiling with his eyes and tapping out an uncertain rhythm with his foot, at each face, at each pair of shoes that was either work boots or gym shoes, or feather-scuff wing-tips, at an entire orchard of hands that were capping knees or trembling with cigarettes, or thumbing a book, or gnarled into a shape like a walnut, he felt break open inside him a kernel of love so sudden and so total that, at first, it frightened him.

With an aching heart
And a worried mind.

It frightened him because he knew what he was about to do.

There was no name for what he was feeling. After the first fright, it settled in him like a medical fact. He could not have stopped it now if he had wanted to stop it, and there was nothing in him now that wanted to stop it.

His foot began to tap out the time. It was a time all his own, and he noticed that, for once, he was not hearing the clicking of the valve, that the only beat he could hear was the one he made with his own muscle and nerve.

The kid was stroking back his hair, shaking his head, and scanning, back and forth, the line of waiters.

He wondered: Is this what happens to the young people now? His own scuffling sons crowded at the back of his mind.

He kept tapping, louder now, humming without knowing the tune, watching patients on their way to the recreation hall, the nurse at her note pad, and the slick motion of the wheeling orderlies.

She called his name. Still tapping, he waited. She called his name again. He waited, still tapping, until the timing was right. Then he stood.

"Look," he said. He sat down in the chair beside her desk. "I don't want no more pills."

"Here," she said.

He pushed the thermometer away. "I said, I don't want no more pills."

"I can't help that. The doctor has prescribed..."

"Listen to me." He was crowded with an urge to convince her. Or if not her, then anyone who could hear him. And although he could not see them, he knew that the others were watching, and that if they couldn't hear, then they were studying what it was he might be saying. "Listen," he said, "You got to know what these pills do to a person."

"But they're for..."

"I know what they're for. And I know what they do."

"Mr. Martin, could you please..."

"You see that kid over there?" He nodded behind him. "Now what kind of junk have you got him on?"

"We can't discuss another patient's medication."

"That's cause you don't want people to know what's..."

"Look." She pecked her finger on the table in front of his arm. "I'm just a flunky here like anybody else. I don't make any decisions about how anybody gets treated or who gets what or how much of it or why or who gets to know what. All I get to do is do my job and you're not helping any."

"Well, who does decide?"

"Your doctor."

"Well, that's what I wanted to know."

•   •   •

At work, in the hustle of hotcakes, coffee, biscuits and gravy, eggs and fried potatoes, in the steam and grease of cooking she simmered over what she felt was coming, snapping at customers and worrying over change until she could wonder no more. *I've spent half my life waitin to see what move he was gonna make next,* she thought. *So he can make whatever move he wants. I'm just gonna do what I got to do.*

•   •   •

They said that when he left the clinic, there was a fierce cloud across his face, but that once he left his argument with the doctor and started to the pharmacy, the look on his face was one of relief, as if he had just been freed of some task, or had beaten some charge, or had won some secret victory.

At the pharmacy, they said he came up to the counter and leaned across a formica top and looked over the shelving and examined how the thin metal uprights were fastened to ceiling and floor and how the shelves set on slender brackets shaped like the wings of birds. As he stared with his elbows on the counter, the pharmacist asked him, as usual, for his slip, and when he acted as if he had forgotten it, the pharmacist, in his turn, forgot him.

• • •

The pharmacist was getting drowsy over the order forms. What was stocked and what needed to be stocked had blurred in memory and his eyes crossed themselves to muddy the lines and letters.

Sometimes, when he was driving, the same thing happened. Under the tedium of sun and pavement, his eyes would dive together, his head would lean into oblivion, the lanes of traffic would merge, and he would fall into that half-state that leads into sleep or into death.

When he heard the crash, he shook himself, as he would out of that highway stupor, and for a moment, he reached for a steering wheel that wasn't there. What he felt instead was the tabletop, and as his eyes uncrossed, he placed himself again in the pharmacy among the pills and lotions and salves and capsules and potions and tablets and cylinders of gelatin and powders, among the bottles, jars, pouches, envelopes, and trays, the shelves and drawers, the scales and spoons, mortar and pestle and bunsen burner, and to note it all, the forms, the pens, and typewriters, and to study it all, the manuals, books, booklets, tracts, magazines, and pamphlets. Among the shine of porcelain, glass, formica, and floorwax. In the smell of alcohol.

Again the crash. He stood and turned, and saw a white cloud of plaster rising up out of the stacks and heard the rain of bottles and tablets, so he ran to the end of the shelves that, with a final wobble, had just gone over.

How did he get back here? The patient who had lost his

prescription, who had come to the counter grinning some secret joke, was standing in the pillshamble wreckage of the shelves, testing the next row with one hand, and rubbing at his chest with the other.

"What the hell are you doing?" He shouted, and the man looked up. *Where's security?* he thought. *Any guy who can tear down those shelves...* he stopped. The man was leaning, not pushing, on the shelves now. His free hand was pulling across his chest as if he wanted to pull apart his ribs.

He can't breathe, thought the pharmacist, stunned and wordless. The man looked to him. Behind the mask of his grin, a flood of pain had welled up into his eyes. The man looked once more over the wreckage of the shelves, then, still grinning like a winner, he toppled.

●　　●　　●

She took her break in a back booth before the lunch rush. The counterman leaned back against the carving board and began to sharpen his knife on a rod, flashing and ringing the blade in a wickering motion. Pride flickered like a tear in the corner of his eye.

Her coffee was still too hot to drink, so she looked out across the booths and past the counterman to the window dimmed with steam. She felt better now. *Workin's good for you,* she thought. *It clears your mind.* She felt ready for what was coming on, for what she could almost hear: a long-travelled, high and lonesome note. Behind the window and its haze of steam she could see the shapes of a pair of old men, the stalled shapes of the traffic, and behind the traffic, the apartment houses in their ranks.

The counterman stopped to examine the bright eye of the knife, then went on with his sharpening. The steel rang and warbled in time with his stroke.

She picked up her coffee, closed her eyes, and saw what she already knew she would see: a house gone windowless and grey: she was waiting in the middle of a road before a house gone windowless and grey. The dark porch was crowded with desertion. A voice wailed in every nailhead, a bent note twisted from every warped plank. Where were those voices gone? Where were the voiceless? She listened: From down the long road she felt a shudder

70

of on-coming motion like a train. It came closer and her heart pounded with a swift steel clatter. The motion surrounded her with a muscular rumble. It gripped her like labor, pressed her temples like a grief, pushed her through the channel of a dark and steady drumming, then released her, choking with knowledge and blinded with tears and windowlight.

The counterman had finished his knife and its ringing noise of steel.

She brushed back her tears. They would call her soon enough about Randall. But she knew it was already over.

She would have to call his brothers and his sisters and her own kin, long-distance, to all the states where they had scattered. She would have to sign papers, make arrangements, take on new bills. But for now, she wanted to calm herself, to make herself ready, and to finish out the day.

Her sons wrestled forward in her mind. In the map she was drawing for them, the roads and broad rivers wandered like veins.

Five Stories

New Burnisht Joys
Which yellow Gold and Pearl Excell!
Such sacred Treasures are the Lims in Boys,
In which a Soul doth Dwell;
Their Organized Joynts and Azure Veins
More Wealth include, then all the World contains.

Thomas Traherne
The Salutation, 4

Four Boys on the Corner

Main Street was dark as the face of a sleeper. From where Lonnie sat, he could see the dark-lidded eyes of Topper's and Wanda Bear's and he could hear, from Wanda Bear's, the tub-thump heartbeat sound of the bass guitar as it pulsed through the walls. Whenever the door opened, he could hear the rattlebasket sound of the drums, the wiry picking of the lead guitar, and the high yodeling voice of the lead singer in his Hank Williams, Elvis, and Chuck Berry. And he knew that, with each of the old songs, the women would be gathered in the middle of the floor to do their clog-dance, two-by-two, old and young, their arms spread wide like broad-winged circling birds.

But Lonnie and the others were barred out. The police had been checking all the bars and demanding IDs. Two years, three years more for each of them before they could legally get in. It was a hill-billy band anyway, and only sometimes did they play rock.

A spread quilt of houselights and streetlamps hung around them, but the forty mouths of the stores and storefront churches of Main Street were shut. So they were alone on Main Street with the darkness, the light patches, and the steadythump sound of Wanda Bear's hillbilly band.

A small wind passed down the row of three and four-story buildings with the nested apartments above each dark storefront. It pushed at the dust of the sidewalks and the litter of the gutters and the papers full of daily news that wrapped themselves around the parking meters and the tires of the parked cars. The wind was just strong enough to push a can in a slow rattle down the white line of Main Street, and was just strong enough to swing the hanging sign of the boarded-up Mount Nebo Baptist Church and to make the sign's ironparts creak together with a sound like desertion.

Lonnie and three others were sitting on the steps of the church, shrouded by its plywood frame.

Jimmy got up to leave and Lonnie watched him. First he brushed the dust from his elbows, then from the back of his jeans. Then he pulled his collar high around his neck, stuck his hands in his pockets, stepped out to the middle of the sidewalk, turned halfway back to the others and said, "Catch you later."

Harold laughed. His laugh was hard as a diamond. Jimmy had already gone to the corner and turned toward his house, though they all knew that wasn't where he was going, when Harold stood and mocked, "Hey man, bring me back some money."

Jimmy had turned the corner. Either he had not heard or he was trying not to hear, for he made no response that Lonnie could hear. Harold went to the corner and, with the lights from Wanda Bear's flashing weakly in his face, lanced a sneer at Jimmy's back. "Hey man," he called.

"Let him alone," Lonnie called.

Harold laughed again. He stood with his arms folded, glaring at Jimmy's back. The matchflame flicker of a sneer burnt out, and he turned to look out onto Main Street.

Bobby stood and walked to Harold's side, looked once in Jimmy's direction, then turned in a slow circle to take in Wanda Bear's and Topper's, the closed faces of the storefronts, the house-lights, the streetlamps, the parked cars, and the lights that led down Main Street to downtown and the river. All this in his wide-eyed angeldust stare. Then he said, "Come on man, let's get out a here."

"Where you goin?" Harold said.
"Come on."

"You comin?" Harold turned to Lonnie, still on the steps, still leaning back in the darkness, watching their faces as the dim lights moved across them, thinking *I don't want no part of what Bobby's got in mind, not when he looks that way.*

"Hey man, you comin?" Harold asked.
Lonnie shook his head.
Harold struck his grin again. "You gonna make some money too?"
"No man," Lonnie said, "I aint gonna make no money."

"Come on," Bobby said, slapping Harold back-handed across the shoulder. He hadn't ever looked at Lonnie. "Come on," he said once more to Harold, and Harold nodded once to Lonnie as they turned.

The two crossed Main, and Lonnie watched as Bobby led Harold along the side of a building and into the alley and the alley's darkness.

Main Street was dark as the sleeping face of his grandmother. An hour before, as he had left the house, he stood by her bed a moment, in the kitchen where they had set her up when she first came to stay with them. He watched her in the light of the stove pilots. She lay with her mouth open, breathing like a cougar, her eyes clamped shut as if she were working at it, the wrinkles behind her eyes stitched fine as the tip of a hawk's feather, her fist gripping the corner of her blanket, the black cables of her hair thrown across her pillow like tow lines.

Old woman of the coal camps.

He was thinking as he watched Harold and Bobby turn the corner into the alley, Harold waving his arms to tell some story, Bobby stiff as a lamppost. He was thinking *She's layin there dyin right now, and these fools....* He stopped himself. They were his friends.

And what could they do to change her dying? She was gone, even though everybody pretended she was only sick. With every breath her lungs rattled like she'd thrown a rod. He knew what that rattle meant, and so did they all. But no one would say it. They took her every day to burn out her cancer under some nightmare machine, but it was just a torture. She never said so, but he knew. She carried the pain like a purse clutched close to her chest. She was gone.

He watched her. He knew she knew. How could she keep from knowing?

The door swung open at Wanda Bear's. He could hear the band playing Wildwood Flower and he knew that the women were dancing their bird-like dance and even some of the men had joined and all of them who were at other times mechanics or barmaids or construction hands or kitchen help or had no jobs at all and who sometimes cheated on each other or had shirt-ripping, eye-gouging fights or drank up each other's money or talked trash on each other were now either clapping at the sides or joining in the dance like wide-winged birds.

Then the door swung shut.

Lonnie stood up almost as if the swinging door had tripped a spring in him and took three steps before he began to think about where he was going, and even as he began to think about where he was going he was already walking straight down Main Street past the laundromat, the Chinese man's store, and Chubb's Furniture where tomorrow he would work carrying refrigerators and living room sets up the narrow hallways into apartments out of which he would someday soon carry them back down once people couldn't make the payments.

And he had gotten nearly to Thirteenth before he stopped, thinking *If I go much further down it's all coloreds.* But he didn't want to go back. What could he go back to do? Stand outside the bar and wait for the door to swing open? Go back to the house to listen to his Granny's lioness breathing and watch her dying cell by cell?

There would be no finding Bobby and Harold and he didn't want to find Jimmy. So there was nothing for him to do but to study the dark face of Main Street at this silent end, away from the other boys and away from Wanda Bear's heartbeat walls.

But here all he heard was the rattling of his grandmother's lung, a sound that filled his ears with ashes and raised up his nerves as if a file were working on them.

He began to shake his head, trying to shake off the hand that held the file, trying to shake loose the ashes. He was thinking *Aint no way for me to ever get no rest,* thinking already of the lifting and sweating he had for tomorrow and how he would try to sleep tonight in the room next to her and how after the younger kids were quiet and the TV off there would still be her croupish growl that the doctors would never be able to burn away, the growl that even now was in his ears just as sure as if he were still standing over her, as if he now could hear her clamp shut her eyes and net up her wrinkles fine as feather and flare her nostrils like a mare and shake the corner of her blanket in the hard grip of her small fist.

A police car slowed to study him and he stared his hatred back at the driver, thinking *If you mess with me right now I'll do somethin crazy.* The car went on.

Looking down Thirteenth toward Vine, Lonnie watched the traffic lights do their slow dance of colors, all in a line. Cars and people moved across the intersection at Vine, two blocks away. But as Lonnie looked up Main, across the storefronts and into the windowed apartments, he saw nothing moving until he sat down in the vault-shaped doorway of the closed-down bank and pulled out his knife to whet it on the marble of the step. He heard a window slide open and looked up to the third floor of the building on the corner. A girl in a housecoat stepped out onto the fire escape, bare-footed and cautious. Her left hand stayed across her breast to keep the housecoat clasped around her, and she walked to the end of the railing, leaned over with her right hand stretched out, and rapped three times on the nearest window of the building next door. She turned, brushed a loose strand of hair back out of her eye and looked down at the street where he sat thinking *Does she see me?*

She made no sign. She stepped back through her window and waited. In a moment her friend opened her window and they began to talk, window to window, framed in the houselights below them. Lonnie was too far below and they were talking too softly for him to know what they said, but by the time he had whetted down his knife, tested the blade, closed it, and put it in his pocket, the girl's friend had gone from her window and he realized that the girl in the housecoat had been watching him all along and that she was watching him now. She let down her hair and it fell in a dark rope down her shoulder, and he slowly stood, not wanting to seem too anxious, thinking *How can I make her talk to me? What do I say?*

But as soon as he stood, she smiled a hint of a smile, and with the hand that held the housecoat together made a hint of a wave. Then she closed the window.

By now, the only breathing that he heard on silent Main Street was his own.

He had to work tomorrow. It was time to be home.

The Fountain

When she came out at the head of the alley she stopped with her arms straight down at her sides, her purse in her left hand, her clean jaw white under the streetlamp, the small gold pin at her collar tinselling dimly. She looked once to the left, then to the right; down Vine toward downtown and Kentucky and the river, up Vine toward the hills. Behind her, between the black walls of the alley, the broken glass of the alley floor glittered in the lamplight.

Across the street, Harold leaned into the restaurant's doorway and said, "She's out there now."

Jimmy was at the counter with a cigarette. "What's she doin?"

Harold looked out to the street. "She's just standin there right now."
"What's she got on?"
"Goddamn it, come on out."

Jimmy ran the stub of the cigarette into the ashtray, pushed himself up from the counter, flicked his hair back out of his eye, shrugged his jacket collar high up on his neck, and followed Harold out the door and onto the street.

She was blocked for a moment by a stopped bus. "Where is she?" Jimmy said.

"Wait a minute." Harold hooked his thumbs into his belt and backed against the wall. "Wait a minute," he said. She hadn't gone. They would have seen her on the bus if she'd gotten on. The bus snarled, broke into traffic, and gassed itself past her. They saw her then crossing the street toward them, looking to the left and to the right without seeing either of the boys. Her arms were still at her sides and she held her shoulders squared back. They rocked back and forth as she walked. Her close-cropped hair was dark under the wide brim of her hat. Her unbuttoned collar was close on her neck, but her shirt was open three buttons down and the gap spread wide by her shoulders. Her ankles and hands and open chest were white.

"Shit," Jimmy whispered.

She stepped between the two parked cars and onto the curb, then stopped and looked, past the two standing boys, up the street. The boys could see, behind her, the brighter Vine below them. Where they stood, there was only the street-lamp, the restaurant's neon, and the glitter of broken glass.

One old man in a heavy black coat with a black bundle in his crossed arms walked the opposite sidewalk and watched the three standing in the restaurant's pool of red neon.

Jimmy reached to his pocket for a cigarette; Harold looked away. On the curb, by the parking meter, in the dim neon of the sign and the restaurant's window, she stood, her arms at her sides, her face turned to her right shoulder, her eyes on some hidden thing far up the street. Then she turned with an abrupt and intentional twist of the hips and headed down the long street toward downtown. They watched her swing in and out of shadow as she walked.

"Weird," Jimmy said.

"I told you didn't I?"

"Give me a cigarette." Jimmy had found none in his own pocket.

Harold handed him the pack. "She goes around here like that all the time," he said.

"It's weird. Is it a him or a her?"

"Both."

"What?"

"She's half man, half woman."

"Shit."

"It's the truth."

Jimmy lit his cigarette, drew deeply on it, and muttered out the smoke. He was looking at the street, toward the alley from which she had come. "How do you know he ain't just dressin like that?"

"They told me."

"Who told you?"

"Those guys that live up here."

"What did they tell you?"

"She's half man, half woman."

"How's she gonna be that when you gotta be born one or the other?"

"She was born a man."

79

"Well then she's a man. Supposed to be."

"They say he was rich. And then he had a car accident. The doctor says, Look, the way I gotta sew you up, you're either gonna be a woman or you're gonna be nothin."

"Shit."

"It's the truth."

The old man had stopped. He had leaned against the doorpost of a storefront and was holding his bundle as a woman might a child, his forearms crossed, the bundle pulled in close to the hollow of his body. He was watching the concrete and the cigarette butts and the dim lightnings of the shivered glass as if he expected them to move. His shoulders were caved in like a broken axle, his body arced under the black coat like the unseen crescent of the nearly full moon.

Out of some window above the black and empty storefronts two sudden voices leapt, twisted in rage, dropped to the street, and died.

"Let's get out a here," Jimmy said.

"Where you gonna go?"

"I just want to get out a here."

"I aint goin anywhere."

Jimmy stepped out from the wall, left his cigarette burning in the corner of his mouth, pulled his four-inch Barlow from his pocket, held the knife handle in his right hand, took the blade between forefinger and thumb of his left hand, then whipped both hands so that the blade broke out. Then, more slowly, he folded the blade back in. He turned. "You say she can fight?"

"You seen them arms of hers. She could break somebody in half."

Jimmy kicked the parking meter and the change and mechanics chinked inside it. "Aint no cop will mess with her," Harold said. "She'll beat the hell out of em. She whipped three of em one night."

Jimmy closed the knife and ran it back into his pocket, then backed himself up to a parked car, leaned back, spat, and said, "She looked like she had tits."

"That's cause she's got all them muscles. Couple boys up on Main thought they'd cut open her shirt one night and show she didn't have any tits. She put em in the hospital. Cracked their ribs. But she had them big muscles, so she looked like she had em."

80

"Shit."

"You ask em down on Main."

The old man had disappeared. They were alone on Vine Street but for the passing buses and cars and the people in the restaurant and the red noise of a siren on some other block.

"Let's get out a here," Jimmy said.

"Where you wanta go?"

"Over on Main."

"Well go on."

Jimmy pushed himself up from the car, ran his hair back out of his eyes, put his hands in his pockets, and kicked the base of the parking meter. "Where's she go?" he said.

"They say she goes down on the Fountain with the queers."

"Do they pay her?"

Harold spat. "I don't know," he said. "I don't know nothin about that stuff."

•   •   •

Out on Main, a woman, her long hair mantling her shoulders, leaned out of a second-floor window and watched the pair of cops with their sticks under their arms as they checked the dark store-fronts. One, with a flashlight, stopped every couple doors and ran his light for a moment into the emptiness, then walked on. She followed them down to where they had parked their car, and after they had re-entered it and started it, she followed them back up the street to where they had not seen Jimmy in the darkness of the vest-ibule of the Mount Nebo Baptist Church. He was watching the street, his elbows on his knees, his hands cupped around the last cigarette he had. He saw her look down at him in his darkness. The blue light of a television flickered behind her. She leaned down to catch him better, cocked her head oddly at him, then withdrew.

He was thinking: *That was ten dollars that he give me. Ten Dollars!* In a park, in the drowned green darkness where the man had parked his car. He had a memory of blue: the thick veins of his young manhood, the glassy tendons of the man's hands. It was all a shock. The man's hands cupped his groinparts and raised them turbulent and strained. Then the man's head dropped and started working him, and the boy's gut started to crawl up into his chest and his legs went sick and weak, and he watched, amazed, the thick hair in his lap rocking back and forth as the man mumbled over him, and as his body, like the body of somebody else, some stranger, went through its work. His turbulence billowed and built, then broke like a cup. The man lifted himself, then brought the boy's head down with his glassy hands onto his chest, and Jimmy felt the slow breath and beat of the man's chest and felt the dead recoil in his own.

He smoked the cigarette down til the coal began to heat his fingers and the smoke turned bitter. Then he threw the butt out into the street and saw the coal split, rage, and die. It was late. *I might as well get on down there*, he thought. *There aint nothin here to wait for.* He stood and jerked his jacket collar close on his neck. *It's ten dollars*, he thought. Then he started to walk.

● ● ●

Down on the Fountain, near the concrete block of stairs that led into the glass face of the buildings, she stood, her chest open and full, her hands on her hips, her hip cocked, watching the people on the wide square, in a circle singing. They had guitars, two of them, and their heads rocked all at once for a time. Then the circle broke, and the people joined hands and began to move around the guitarists in a ring. They danced like that til one of them fell, then they waited for her to stand and began to dance again.

Behind them, the green woman of the Fountain showered white water out of her hands and onto her farmers and women molded below her.

She saw the boy at the side, by one of the trees, leaning against its concrete tub, his hands in his pockets, his jacket collar high on his neck, his hair in his eye, his eye on the dancers, his mouth set solemnly, his body tight against the base of the tree. A tall thin man in a blue jacket stood behind him.

Outside the Church

The two boys waited, leaning against the fender of a truck, facing the door of the Main Street Free Pentacostal Church as the rattle-shack rattleshack of the tambourine simmered to a stop and the broad piping of the organ swelled to a close and the woman singing put the feathers and flurries on the end of her song, and they listened in the lamplight dimness until the full-bellied final words of the preacher were spoken and the service was over, sudden like a book snapping shut, and they watched as the people of the church filed out of the church's storefront that used to be the pool-hall, across the dimness of the sidewalk, and into the church's recreation hall storefront that used to be the laundromat. When the people switched on the lights, the hall brightened with balloons and a Pepsi machine. The men were in their white shirts and suitcoats and narrow ties and held their Bibles clamped in their hands. The women wore their hair piled incredibly on top of their heads and wore bright skirts that went to their knees and held their Bibles each against her breast. The children were bright and stiff in their suits and ribbons.

She was among the children, helping keep them in line along the dark path of those few feet of sidewalk between the two store-fronts, awkward in her black stiff shoes.

Behind her came the line of a dozen children. To her right and left were a group of men and a group of women who had stopped to talk, each in their own small circle. As she passed between them, a narrow bar of light from a turning car at Fourteenth crossed her, and as it crossed her the light touched on her face, the points of her breasts, her hands that touched the shoulders of the children, and the belt and knee-capping hemline of her skirt. Her hair was still short, and it fell across her brow and it brushed her shoulders.

"Hey Jeannie," Bobby called.

She looked just short of where the boys stood, then back to the church door. The woman at the end of the line of children nodded her forward.

Bobby laughed. "Hey Jeannie," he called, "Let's go out tonight."

The girl had already gone into the brightness of the recreation hall. The woman spoke to the gaping children, "It's all right. You just ignore these street punks."

Bobby laughed again. "You fat ass bitch," he muttered, just loud enough that she would hear. The group of church men had turned. The biggest of them carried no Bible. He had blond crew-cut hair and he swung his long arms for the exercise as he stood and talked and popped his gum.

Lonny saw him watching Bobby. "Come on," he said. "Let's get out a here."

"She's still a fox," Bobby was saying. He was watching the door of the recreation hall for a glimps of her, and as he watched, he popped his knuckles, one knuckle at a time.

"She's run away four times before," Bobby said. "She'll run away again."

"Yeah. But she never been in the church before."
"Hell, she ran around and got high just like everybody else."
"Yeah, but now she's got saved."
"I'll show her how to get saved, man."
"You ain't gonna show her much of anything as long as she's with that bunch of people."

Bobby snickered. The grin on his face stayed, but something new was behind it so it was like a grin made of plaster. "Fuck that bunch of people," he said.

"That's probably what they're sayin to you."

"Hey man," he gestured like someone making a dare, "they aint sayin nothin to me. They aint sayin nothin."

He popped three knuckles, slowly, one after another, watching the blond-haired man and the smaller men standing in their circle of discussion. Then he looked from the circle of men to the circle of women. And spat.

"They aint sayin nothin to me. At all."

Quick as a house of cards falls, his grin was gone. He'd popped his last knuckle. Of a sudden, he pushed himself up from the truckfender, grabbed a parking meter, swung himself against it, and said, aloud so that the children who stood in the door with their Pepsis would hear it:

84

"This bunch of people aint sayin nothin to me, cause they aint nothin but an *ignorant* bunch of motherfuckers."

The circle of women froze. The children calmly drank their Pepsis. The blond man took two steps out of the circle of men with the leather stride of a cop and said, "Boy," he raised a finger, "you got a bad mouth."

"I didn't say nothin to you."

"I don't care who you're sayin it to. It's who you're sayin it around."

"I didn't say nothin to you."

The circle of women broke apart and turned to the recreation hall, sweeping the children ahead of them.

"Boy, you better shut up." He was shaking a large finger toward Bobby's face.

"Hey, you better watch what the fuck you're sayin."

The man looked over to the children to see if they heard. Then he looked back to Bobby, shaking the finger more slowly. "I said you better shut up."

"And who are you?"

"I'm *me*."

Bobby snickered. The door slammed shut behind the children. The blond man looked side to furied side as one of the others whispered at his ear. He raised his hands into half-fists. Another of the men came up at his other side and muttered into his other ear.

Bobby stepped up, flipping back his yellow hair. He stood ready, one fist cradled in the other, a sneer flickering in his left nostril, a new grin flickering at the right side of his mouth.

Then the man dropped his hands. "Come in," he said to the others. "I know where we can find a phone."

The three men turned their backs on the boys and stomped into the recreation hall.

Bobby laughed again. "Chickenshit," he said. He turned, walked quickly to the vacant lot at the corner, searched in the weeds, picked up a brick half, and came back with it to the front of the church. He was walking slowly this time, as if he had no particular thing on his mind. He held the brick palmed up, as a boy does to hide a cigarette in the cup of his hand.

He knew which car. The sales lot sticker was still in the window. Lonnie watched as Bobby stepped up, flipped his wrist, and turned.

The window collapsed with a sound like a flower opening, if a flower opened in an instant. The broken glass hit the sidewalk with a snap like a string of beads.

"That'll show em not to fuck with me," Bobby said, flipping back his yellow hair.

Lonnie had seen it. T-Bone had seen it. All the Shortfields had seen it. The boy with the limp had seen it. All of T-Bone's kids had seen it. But after the police car came around and they called Bobby over to the car, no one would answer when they asked, Did you see him hit that window?

Everybody looked at everybody else and T-Bone looked straight at the cops and shook his head from side to side. Not a word was said.

But they took Bobby anyway. He argued at them and waved his arms and pointed both hands to himself, but the church people pointed and insisted and finally the cops put Bobby against the car, searched him, cuffed him, and took him away.

T-Bone said, "Now if he'd of busted out my window, I wouldn't call no cop. I just would of shot him between the eyes. I'd give him a gun, just to make it even, and I'd of told him, Now I'm gonna shoot you. I wouldn't call no cop."

The church people had begun to leave for their cars. Lonnie watched them paying their respects, each to the preacher and each to each.

Respect, Bobby always said, is the name of the game.

They'll Kill You Harold

Over the chain fence that blocked the back porch and the brick-cobbled yard from the alley, across the vacant yard beside the warehouse with its broken bricks and black weeds, under the blue span of the street lamp, out on the street, the two could see the red eruption of the squad car's light, the two cops, and the man from the car they had stopped. The red light ran across the walls and through the weeds and touched the faces of the boys where they stood, watching.

Harold spat, clean into the alley. He spat hard, and the sound he made was almost like a cough. He kept his tight body pressed close against the fence, propped with his elbows hooked forward, the fencetop in his armpits. He was knocking his knuckles together, watching. Small rags of the red light caught on the brass of the medals he had found for his jacket. The cops had the man between cars, and they stood on each side of him. The man moved his arms weakly up and down as he talked, but the cops kept their hands on their belts. One of them had a clipboard under his arm. Harold's tap, one knuckle against another, followed, in a way, the pulse of the bleeding squad car's light. But sometimes he missed a beat; sometimes he fell behind.

"You got a cigarette?" he said.
"No," Jimmy said. "I aint got a cigarette."

Harold spat again, silently, precisely. Jimmy had his arms spread and both hands clutched the fencetop. The fence ran across the back yard of Jimmy's mother's building and separated the yard from the alley. The gate, to their left, hung loose because the latch was broken. When there was a heavy wind, the gate banged back and forth across the broken latch. But there was no wind. The cop's light, quick as blood, quicker than any wind, cut across the empty warehouse lot and all over the boys and the walls and brick cobbles of the yard and the chain fence. Out on the street, pinned by the same light, the man between the cops bent down and lifted his trunk lid. One of the cops looked in.

"Jimmy," Harold said. "You got a cigarette?"
"No," he said. "I'm out of cigarettes."

87

Harold stopped the drumming of his knuckles then, and brought his hands under his chin. The movement stretched the denim of his jacket and stretched the bright patch sewn across the back. The cops had the man stretched over the hood of the squad car now, his arms spread out to hold himself up. The cop with the clipboard took notes while the free cop frisked the man. Over and again, the red light slashed across the three of them, shredded over the walls, broke across the three blank yards and along the wall of the warehouse, and found the faces of the two watching boys. The man on the hood was still talking, but the cops said nothing. The free cop finished his search, and the cop with the clipboard finished his writing, so they took their man, cuffed him, steered him around the car, opened the door, and shoved him in the back seat. They took their own places, shut off the light, and drove off.

"Let's go down to Vine Street," Harold said.

"What's down on Vine Street?"

"You know what's on Vine."

"There's nothin on Vine."

"Let's go to Vine Street."

"Harold, you doin pills?"

"Go to hell."

Harold began to tap his knuckles again, one against another. He drew his fists back slowly each time, and rapped them together so that Jimmy could hear each crack. "Let's go down to Vine Street," Harold said.

"What you want to do on Vine Street?"

"I'm gonna kill me a nigger."

"Sure."

"I swear I will." He stopped the tapping, but kept his fists pressed close together.

"Sure."

"I had enough."

"Enough what?"

"They been pushin me. I tell you man they been pushin me. I ain't gonna take it any more."

Jimmy spat this time. He turned around, leaned backwards against the fence, and looked up into the skinny tree that broke up through the bricks in his mother's yard and whose roots had lifted some of them like hills. "They'll kill you," he said.

"I ain't afraid of any niggers."

88

"They'll kill you Harold."

"What do I care if they kill me. I can stomp their ass."

"You're doped up Harold."

"I aint scared of no niggers. I got a knife. I got my hawk blade."

Jimmy turned again, back toward the street, and stood with his arms on the fencetop, his fingers tapping on the chain.

"You know what happened today?" Harold asked.

"What happened?"

"They jumped me."

"Who jumped you?"

"Three of em. I got one of em. They cut me up."

"Where at?"

"Up on Milton. There was four of em. I was comin down the hill and they come out of some old garage over by the stairs comin down the hill and they tried to get me to give em some money and I told em to go to hell so they started to get me all at once. Did I show you where they cut me:" Harold opened his jacket, lifted his shirt, and shifted to get into the light. There were four wounds, each four inches long. They were pink, freshly scarring, lipped like mouths. At the rim of each was a crust of blood.

"You know who did it?" Jimmy asked.

"I know em. There was one caught me from behind and held me, and one come up and I kicked him in the nuts, and the other one started to cut on me til that old man that lives up there on top of the garage come out and scared them off. But I got one of em."

"You got one?"

Harold reached into his pocket, pulled out the knife, and opened the beaked blade. He held it in the light. It was white where the metal was polished, black where the blood had dried. "That's fresh," he said.

"I thought you said they was all run off."

"That was before they grabbed me. I got him good. I'm gonna get the rest of em tonight."

"Go ahead and get em."

"You gonna come?"

Jimmy spat, walked over to the steps of the porch, and sat down. Harold turned back to the fence, hooked his elbows over again, and began to pick at the knuckles of his left hand with the knife.

89

"Jimmy. I said, Are you gonna come?"

"You don't know what nigger it was."

"I don't care."

"They'll tear you apart on Vine Street."

"You think I'm scared of them?"

"They'll kill you Harold. You're too little."

"I'll get em one at a time." He was concentrating on his knuckles; the skin across the tops of them was white. In a couple more scrapes, he drew beads of blood.

"You're doped up Harold," Jimmy said from the steps.

"Fuck you."

Jimmy kicked out from the steps, flew across the few feet to where Harold stood, grabbed Harold's collar with one hand, and pulled the other back in a fist. He had the momentum, so he ripped Harold away from the fence and backed him for a couple more feet, then shoved him away and started to say, Watch your damn mouth Harold, but Harold cut through his words, shortly, sharply, "Don't *fuck* with me Jimmy." He had his footing then and he had the knife flung back. They stood, one matching the other, and Jimmy said, "I aint scared of your goddamn knife Harold." And Harold said, more slowly, "Don't fuck with me."

He brought the knife down, held it for a moment in his open palm, then closed it and put it back into his pocket. "You think I'm scared?" He said. "You think I care?" He turned around, found the gate in his path, kicked it so that it banged against the latch piece and clattered the chain all up and down the fence, waited for it to rebound and swing clear, then walked out into the alley.

Jimmy let his fist down then. Harold was headed across the back yard towards Vine. Jimmy caught the light off the patches and badges Harold had collected for his jacket and thought of how he had let Harold go like that. He doubled his fist again, batted at the fence as he stared, then turned around when he heard his name called.

It was Lonnie. "What's goin on?" Lonnie said.

"Harold's doped up again."

"Where'd he get to?"

"He took off."

"Was he messin with you?"

"He thought he was."

"He's crazy. Every time he gets doped up, he starts messin with people."

"Every time you say somethin to him, he says I don't care."
Jimmy remembered when Harold got the tattoo—there was a boy
over on Main who cut tattoos. The boy hit a vein, and blood began
to run stripes down Harold's arm. "I don't care," Harold had said.
The boy found a cloth to put over the vein and went on cutting the
tattoo. "What do I care?" Harold had said.

"You hear Harold got cut?" Lonnie asked.
"He says some niggers cut him."
"Harold's crazy."

Out on Vine, the neon flared against the traffic. Harold could
see it from where he sat, on the stone step of a shattered house on a
side street half a block away. People and cars crossed and recrossed
down on Vine, but Harold's street was empty and the only light
was that of the neon to the one side and a streetlamp far on the
other corner. His jacket was open and his shirt was unbuttoned.
He watched Vine and the crossing and recrossing people and cars
and tapped the unopened knife, in a slow, unvarying motion, into
his left hand. He heard a quick scuttle of feet behind him, and
watched a boy and girl pass by him headed down toward the neon.
They did not see him on his step, and after they passed, Harold set
the knife down on the stone, rolled up each sleeve of his jacket to
bare his forearms, then picked up the knife and opened it. He held
it like a club in his right hand, with the hook of the blade pointed
inward. He held it and shook it three times as a man might shake
another man by the collar, then he brought it down on the back of
his left forearm. For a moment there was pain but no blood. Then
as he forced the crook of the blade down along the round of his
arm, the pain dulled and the blood crept up against the blade.
Then he pulled the blade away and held it up to catch what light
he could on it, closed and pocketed it, looked once at the stripe
running down his forearm, wrist, and hand, then stood. When he
walked out onto Vine, under the maze of neon and lamps, the
blood was bright on his arm.

91

Blood Root

They don't let up,
they just keep on
beginning again
　　　　—P.J. Laska

1. The Road Back to the City

Lonnie stood at the top of a hill, where the road curved behind him to the right. He had stopped and turned to see how far he had climbed up the long slow grade into the ridges, away from the river flats. Against the pasture that climbed toward him, the scattered saplings and thorn trees made hard shadows, and across it, the road curled like smoke. The heat was like a dry bone that you find in the sun, hard, bright, and burnt hollow. The wind brought a smell of drying grass. Beyond the pasture, the river was smooth as slate. Below him, on the ridge-side, the steep bank was thick with cedars and thorn trees, yellow dock and yarrow, and all around him the crickets and locusts seemed to chant out of the thousand blue tops of the Canada thistles.

He heard it before he saw it. At one moment the only sound was the whirring noise of the insects, and at the next was added the deep roar of a car with a ragged muffler and open throttle. And once he saw the car flash over the most distant rise, he watched it begin the long snaking grade toward the top of the hill where he stood.

Mustang, he thought. *Been around awhile*, he could tell by the primer patches that dulled the sun's flash on the body. It fishtailed and cried at the first curve, and then he realized how fast the car must be going. Maybe 80. *He won't want to stop, but if he does it'll be one hell of a ride.*

Peering, he tried to tell if it had Ohio plates. He'd get a longer ride if it did. The nearest bridge was at Maysville, crossing to Aberdeen, so it would be that far at least.

But the sun was shooting straight off the hill at his back, and bumper and grill and windshield gleamed solid gold and blinded out any sign of tags. And then he realized again how fast the car was traveling, for in the gold blindness of the reflected sun, he saw the car leap the last rise, moan over the last curve, and hunger up the white line toward him.

He saw racing stripes and decal patterns on the hood and he thought, *He's a freak, he'll surely pick me up. It's the straight people that pass you up like you're nothin.*

He threw his thumb out at the car, then saw, too late: *That guy's not stoppin for nobody.* So he started to drop his arm and step back when he saw, as the car passed through a patch of shadow and the gold glare went off the windshield, the snaking eyes of the driver and that grin—*like somebody that's pickin a fight with somebody he knows he can whip*—and that sudden copperhead jerk of his hands to the right, and the tight swerve of the car to the right, like a bull in a charge, toward where he stood on the gravel.

His thumb, on its own, closed down over his fist, and he thought, *I'll stand that bastard down.* But he could not stand. The tires spat the first of the gravel at his feet when he jumped, backward and blind so that his feet caught on the wooduseless guardrail, and he fell, shoulder first through the tall weeds, hit the ground, and slid down the bank into the brush.

He was up before the car pulled itself off the shoulder, looking for something to throw: a stick, a rock, a scrap of metal. His hands worked through the weeds and found only gravel, leaves, dry stems of foxtails, while his eyes followed the car up over the curve and out of sight, his voice too choked even to curse.

He reeled a moment, his anger subsiding. Only then did he feel the lurch and spin of his fall and the cool place on his shoulder where his shirt had torn and where the grass and gravel had scraped him. And as he reeled, he felt the thistles he had grabbed instead of the rock he wanted.

Not a hell of a lot you can do, except to know better next time.

He could hear another coming on the highway, but he made no move to climb back up the embankment. *I aint ready for that yet,* he thought, pulling the last of the thistle-spines out of his palm. He sat and listened as the car, an old car by the deep sound of it, shifted gears over the curves, rumbled up the slope, slipped through the gravel above him, rounded the bend, and rumbled and droned away from him. *I've had all I need for awhile.*

He checked the tear in his shirt and brushed the dirt loose off his hip pocket. Then he sat down, reached to the turned-up right cuff of his jeans, and folded the cuff down: It was still there. It had bent a little, and the ends had leaked a few fragments into the cuff, and as he lifted it a seed rolled onto his shoe. But it was still worth lighting up. He hadn't lost that much. He picked the seed off his shoe and pitched it into the·brush. *Maybe I can come back here next summer and find me a good plant. That would be one good thing to come of this.*

That was one of the things Granny had always said: *There's always a way to make some good out of the bad. But Granny aint here to talk about it now. And I aint yet seen what good she got out of all that good.*

But that was something he didn't want to think about yet. A small, nettle-like pain perked up in him at the thought. He folded the joint back into his cuff, stood, turned around to the road, grabbed a handful of fescue and pulled himself up the bank.

2. The Road Down Home

He had walked the last mile. A wordless and sunburnt farmer with feed sacks mounded in his back seat and fragments of grain scattered across the blanket on the front seat had driven him from town. And when he got out, at the foot of the hollow, he stripped off his shirt and tucked it into his hip pocket so he could feel the doubled heat of the sun against his chest as it beat back from the gravel and clay of the road. At the same time he could feel the cool wind he made passing down the narrow channel the road made through the tall weeds and trees.

The sun was near its peak. It pulled from the locusts their highest scream.

The folks already knew. He knew that. But he had been sent. Barney had been sent to Detroit. Johnny to Dayton. Wherever the scattered kin had settled. No messages had been sent, that had all been done by phone. But still they went, each hitch-hiking to some kin. And Lonnie was sent down home.

He had three miles to walk if he took the road, with its twists past three farms, the wrecked tipple, and the store. He thought, *Aint no rides gonna come by here. I know a better way.* And at the culvert built of board and riprap stone, he took the path he knew; up the hill, along the ridge, and down.

He mounted the jumbled stairs of the bed of the run, where the water had broken shelves of the limestone core of the mountain. A thin stream of water ran among the blocks, and sometimes he stepped into a pool and muddied it. The climbing strained the muscles of his stomach in a way he had forgotten, and he felt himself shaping taller and straighter as he walked. The brambles changed for a cedar brake and he could see the biggest cedars that had been felled and left to season for posts and he had to leave the path of the run for one that lay across it. Then he reached the cliffs.

As he climbed, he was looking to either side, into the green patches of frond and leaf that grew up in the shady spaces. He knew what he was after: the broad triple-lobed leaf on the slender stem that sprang from out of the mosses and the ferns and the thousand-flowered floor of the woods, out of the darkest soil in the darkness of the oaks. There was no thought in him that said *I want this*, but he went ahead, searching the green scrolls, plates, fans, and feathers around him, ignoring even the sprig of ginseng until he spotted it, the bloodroot.

He did it the way she had taught him. He had no hoe the way they always had before, but he had his broad-blade Sodbuster knife with the three-inch six-month-in-the-Workhouse blade, so he took it out, opened it, and parted the mosses and black moulder that lay over the soil, then plowed loose the dirt in a circle around the stem, pulling gently until he knew it was loose. Then he pulled free the root, crusted with the black soil, a half-dozen thinner roots shooting off it like hairs. It was as big as his pointed finger. The stem bent sharply where it grew into the root so that as he held the stem upright, the root was level with the ground, and as he turned the stem slowly the pointed finger of the root aimed toward the cliffs, the oaks, and at Lonnie.

Then he rubbed the dirt off the root and he could see the skin, black-red like a hand that has worked on some machine or like his own hand that had dug in the soil.

She had taught him how to hunt the roots. How to tell one from another, how to dig them loose, which ones were good to keep, which ones were good to sell. And she had taught him about bloodroot what had always amazed him:

He snapped it. The flesh of the root was pink, like a fresh cut. Then the small capillary beads formed in a dozen spots across the break. More beads formed, and they pulsed together and flowed

95

brightly off the end of the break and onto his fingers.

"This is a thing that's good for killin pain," she had said. "But only if you use it right. If you use it wrong it's a poison. It's like every other thing that away."

She had stood against the cliffs with him looking down through the trees to where the tipple stood. "You know," she had said, "there's something in the earth that'll cure anything. If you just have the knowledge of it. And if you can get to it."

●   ●   ●

First he saw his cousins leaning into the open hood of the car. He had come out of the woods and back down onto the road and walked through the stunning sun with his eyes down on the road until he felt he was right, and when he looked up his eyes met the bomb-spread darkness of the sycamore and though he saw nothing at first, he heard the clink of tools on an engine and he knew who must be there, and when his eyes adjusted they were already looking back at him, their faces and chests marked with grease, their teeth flashing. James pushed back his hair with the hand that held a wrench. "Hey, Lonnie," he said.

"What's happenin?"
"Aint nothin happenin."
Aint nothin happenin.
"Go on up to the house. They're waitin."

The house: grass fringed the line of faded pickets. He knew the yard before he looked, the red path from the gate to the step, the flower bed made of a tractor tire and crammed with daisies, the sand pile with its buckets and trucks. He heard the call of the children from the creek. Behind the yellow poplar posts, the porch was dark except for the dim channel of light that ran through the screen door, down the hall, to the back window. The red armor of the rooftop threw back the heat. Behind the horse he could see the shimmer of the corn patch, and at the side, in a rank like soldiers, stood the reeling sunflowers.

It was his grandfather's voice: "Hey Lonnie." He wondered, Where did it come from? Where had he been standing? Not in the bare and scorching yard. Then as the porch boards creaked and the old man leaned up from his chair, Lonnie saw the white, arrow-shaped patch where his shirt was open below the neckline. The patch moved up and forward, then sidestepped twice till it was leaning forward at the head of the porch steps, and Lonnie, his eyes adjusting, could see the red lance of his face thrust forward at him.

"Hello boy," he said.

"Hello Papaw." He wouldn't talk to him. Not now, not ever. He started up the steps to get past him, but the old man spoke:

"You can't say she's not better off now. After all that sickness and hardship."

As if he had a right to talk. Lonnie stared at the split grain of the porch step until the old man moved aside. Then he asked, "Where's Phyllis?" That was all he would say.

"She's in the house."

She'd already seen him coming. He didn't know that until he'd stepped into the cool and darkness of the house and that darkness again left him helpless until his sight cleared and he saw her, his aunt, watching from the kitchen doorway, where she had watched him standing on the step with his grandfather. Then she turned and went into the kitchen, saying "How's it in the city, Lonnie?"

She was canning. When he came into the room she was lifting the lid to stir and he smelled the boiling apples and her sweat. She clapped the lid back down and pushed her hand through her short hair. Lonnie shrugged. The pot churned quietly over its blue flame. That was the only light on its side of the room, and so his eye was drawn to the table by the window and to the white way the sunlight ran into the room, whiting out the checkers of the table-cloth and the smoke from the cigarette that, laid at the edge for lack of an ashtray, threatened to burn onto the corner.

Her eye followed his and she went to the table, picked up her cigarette, and sat down. "How's it downtown?" she asked again.

"I got in some trouble," he said. *Why tell her?* he thought. He could trust her, but why tell her? She leaned back against the windowframe and watched him sharp as a knife. She wasn't laughing at him. She wouldn't. He knew that. But her right eye was cocked at him now. In a moment, if he didn't explain, that brow would drop and her left would rise. For fifteen years he had watched those brows cock up and down like switches.

"You know Billy Collins?"

"Yeees"—she drew the word out into a long line of contempt.

"He's been messin with Darlene."

"That's no good. He's strictly no good."

"I knew they was up there. I hollered up at him for him to come down and fight. Wouldn't come."

"He carries a knife, don't he?"

He shrugged, leaned back in the chair and looked out the window to where a path split the thick weeds of the field and opened on the sunflower patch.

"I bet your ma's mad."

"Hell, she wants her to get out a warrant on me."

"What for?"

"Breakin an entrin. I climbed up the fire escape to get in after he wouldn't come down."

"Don find out?"

"He's still got three months. He'll divorce her."

"She oughta know better. He's strictly no good. A girl can get lonesome, but can't go messin around thataway."

He stood, walked over to a shelf, picked up a cigarette, and lit it.

"What do people do that for?" he asked.

Her right eye dropped and her left eye rose like a flag.

"I mean, why do people all the time go messin on each other? I mean, why can't they see? Like Papaw."

Her eye dropped, and she stubbed her cigarette out in a plate and stared away from him. So he knew he had said something wrong, and what was wrong was that he had spoken out against the old man, but he was full of it now, and he wasn't ready to stop.

"I mean," he said, "years ago people didn't do one another like that."

She had picked up the cigarette pack from the table, but she was staring at the stove and the blue flame under the apples, and didn't bother pulling out a cigarette.

"It aint right, is it?" she said.

"Granny don't mean a thing to them people."

"You think so." She sat up straight with the cigarette pack in her right hand and she used it to tap out her words. "You aint fair to people, Lonnie. Years ago people didn't do like people do now. It hurts ever one of em. Papaw and ever one of em."

Lonnie shook his head and turned toward the window. A crow, black as a casket, lit on the head of a sunflower.

98

He sat, thoughtless, watching the crow bob on the sunflower. An unswallowable lump lay in his craw. The crow flew up and around to face the sunflower and flap and hover in front of it to flap and peck out a seed. It dropped toward the ground, choking down the seed, then flapped again, inches from the grass, and flew off.

She tapped him on the arm with her cigarettes. "What you don't know is this: It don't mean nothin for a person to die but that you've lost that one person. And everbody'll go down that road one time. Granny knew it. And she knew that for ever one that's lost there's more to take their place."

He pulled his arm back out of her reach and stared down at the table.

But she wouldn't let him go. "You ask yourself. Did Granny ever put them people down? You ask yourself that." Her brows were set together now like a gunsight. He stood up to get out of their range and walked toward the door.

"Lonnie," she said. He waited. "You don't judge people right."
"You name me one that's got the fight in em Granny had. Look at Papaw."
"You just don't see the fight."

He shrugged. He leaned into the doorway to go, but she spoke, "Lonnie," and he pulled back and leaned his shoulder into the doorframe to wait for her to finish.

"You're not so good yourself, you know." *I don't need to hear this,* he thought. "But it's all the more confused for people now. Just for awhile til people start to movin forward again. It's like a train that starts movin. The cars don't all start forward at once. There's some'll jump forward and some'll roll back till they all start to get the pull and the whole train starts to move in the same direction."

I don't need to hear this.
He pulled himself up to go.

"Lonnie," she said. He waited, feeling her gunsight brow at the back of his brain. "We'll see you Saturday."

He passed down the hall, out the screen door, onto the porch, and into the amazing sun. The boys had taken a break and lay stretched under the tree, their chests pale as the coats of sheep. Papaw was gone. Lonnie turned to look for him, but saw instead the yellow blaze of the sunflowers against the green wall of the woods. He burned to be back on the road.

3. What She Done

muttered and coughed over the stove
    with her cigarette in her mouth
    and served up heaps of ashes and fried potatoes,
blistered the ear of a gun thug
    with a switch of willow,
quilted thick crazy quilts,
    squinting from the smoke of her cigarette
    and shaking loose the ashes,
cursed the landlord with unearthly curses
    so blue and knifish that he forgot to serve the
      notice,
babysat: the dozen grandchildren
    and the nephews, nieces, and various adopteds
    while the others were off to the factory,
    the restaurant, the daylabor, the welfare, the hospital,
lay cursing on the cabin floor with her children
    who were his mother and aunts and uncles
    as the nightriders pitched bullets
    through the coffeepot, the clock, the closet full of clothes,
saw the bleeding of a wound stopped
    and the wound healed
    by the power of words and hands.
carried by her cancer like a fetus
    and burned under the cobalt,
ate matches and spit fire.

4. The Road Back to the City

He'd crossed the bridge to Aberdeen at shift-change and that had gotten him three rides and three towns closer to home. But that time had passed and he was left fifteen miles out on the empty highway in the dark, and he was thinking. *It's either being too wore out or too strung out.* Either way, he'd had it. He could no longer bear to watch the road for headlights. *It's like the time I came off of all that speed:* no muscle, all nerves, he wanted to rest and he wanted to scream. *If I'd been on speed now I'd of walked to Cincinnati six times and back.*

But he wasn't walking. He had come to a dead stop. He couldn't stand to hear for just one more time the clap of asphalt. In spite of everything he could do to get moving, his legs rebelled; they cried and whimpered; they struck.

The locusts rasped from their hidden places. He smelled, from behind the band of trees that hid it, the carp-rot river. A taste, like earth and salt, a taste he had somehow known before, welled along the sides of his tongue.

This is bullshit, he thought. *I got to get back. I'm just tired is all.* But he wasn't; he knew it. He hadn't been walking long enough to be tired. *I must be hungry.* And he was. He hadn't stayed to eat at Phyllis's house, and he'd spent his last money on a lunchmeat sandwich on the way down. So he was hungry. But the nerves of his stomach had pulled together and tightened like the net on a cheese and he knew that not even the half-dozen candybars he had lifted from that last store would do anything but sour him. And he began to think that if he just would sit down to think for awhile that he could get himself straight and get on home. *Just for awhile,* he thought. *Cause I got to get on home.*

But there was no break in the road ahead and the road was tight against the tall summer weeds that were loud with crickets and the weeds were tight against the trees and he wasn't ready to go crashing through the dark brush and down the steep bank to the shore. But he knew a place:

Around the next bend. He had pulled himself enough together to pull himself to the abandoned coal dock he remembered. As he walked he could see the massive and slender iron head of a crane. It peered aslant out of the trees, tall as any of the trees. A shadowy iron latticework ran down its neck like the hatchwork on the skin of a snake. Down to his right he could see the outline of the beached tugboat, its cabin crushed in like a highway beercan or an egg. But he passed these and kept walking until he found the place he wanted, where the wall of thistle and saplings opened. There he mounted the spine of an ancient conveyor and marched over the rubber and canvas that fleshed over its joints, through a forest of sycamores and abandoned winches, toward the bank where the heavy buried rope and iron cables tangled with the roots of the trees, and down off the conveyor and down that bank to the coalyard below the fixed crane: with its long neck, the wide wheel on which it once turned, the pine-sided cab, and its stone mounts, it waited like a quiet hunting bird. Below him, the broken turtle-back of a barge lay cracked and twisted by long years of freezes and thaws and the weight and torment of floods so that it looked as if it had been split and pecked out by a buzzard and left empty at the waterline.

He smelled the sulphur. It had leached out of the coal that carpeted the sloping yard and crystallized so that, here and there among the coal chips, anyone could kick up a piece of bright sulphur that would break in your hands into yellow dust and match-heads.

When he and his cousins fished here, they had carried old tires down onto the sand to burn for warmth and light and to drive away the mosquitoes, and as the tires burned, the crackling smoke that poured out of them smudged their faces. Their poles, propped up on forked sticks, and the lines, running far out into the rippled water, gleamed from the flames.

From the hill, the smoke streaming out of the nest of barges made it seem that the rusted engines had been newly stoked and fired, and what was burning out of the stack was twenty years of decay.

That smoke, with its smell of rubber stronger than a hundred dragstrip starts, was no stronger to him then than the smell of sulphur was to him now. *There's not that much of it here,* he thought, *but I smell it just as strong as if I was in a mine of it.* And the odor welled a wrong taste in his mouth, a taste not all the sulphur, but not something right either.

They had chalked names and pictures and sayings and threats onto the bargewalls with that sulphur. And even now, searching for footholds as he came down the hillside, he could see a face sketched onto the iron. Just a face. No smile or scowl, blank slits for eyes and a straight even line for a mouth. Like a man hungry but not thinking straight on that hunger.

And he felt his own hunger again, the sour undeniable hunger that he knew would only despise the candy in his pockets.

Fuck it: A flood of frustration swept him, and he wondered, *Why in the hell did I get into this anyway? Why in the hell am I out on this damn road so broke I can't pay attention and nothing but this silly candy to feed myself and no way to know when I'll ever get back to town and get a chance to grease and rest my goddamn head?*

And yet he knew there would be no rest at the house, only the fret of family and funeral. They'll all be wondering who gets the furniture and how to pay the bill and there's be some sly dude with slick hands has talked them into a damn silver-lined coffin with gold handles and a naked angel for a head piece.

And he remembered the pine-wood color of her face, her broad Cherokee brow, the hawkfeather wrinkles around her eyes, the cigarette stains around her fingers yellow as calloused and her calloused hard as horn so that she never needed a thimble. And he knew what they would do with her, would gauze her up and pink her face, fill in the cave of her chest, blur her wrinkles, shampoo and fluff her twisty, rope-thick, smoke-colored hair, and drain all her blood and put it in some pot and pump her full of some pink juice. So they could make her into something she never was. And *they* wouldn't understand that these funeral people were ruining her.

Between the railroad tracks and the Ohio River, he remembered she had said. *That's where they put us out, between the railroad tracks and the Ohio River. That was the only place in the state of West Virginia we could go to. And we just lived in tents.* She was just a girl. *And one woman died while we was there. And that's where we had to bury her, where she'd be flooded over ever Spring. And of course we didn't have two flat sticks of wood to put together for a casket. So we just buried her in a bag made out of flour sacks. And now I don't know her people and I don't know the place.*

But it was a place like this, he thought, *like what I just passed through.* A patch of woods thick with flood-trash, in the dark, silt-heavy earth, where her body mouldered freely back into the soil. And maybe floodwashed into this same spot.

And that's the way it ought to be, he thought. None of this waste, and none of this killing off the living for the dead. For as surely as you carried nothing into the world, you will as surely carry nothing out, that preacher said. And the dead don't need to carry nothing, so there's no need to pretend.

And a whole lot of nothin's what she left behind. He regretted the thought, as if he had said it in front of her, as if she were there to hear him and be hurt.

It aint her fault, though. Cause there was nothin she could do. She didn't have nothin to do with it.

But that's what it's all come to:

Nothing: his sister with her whipped head and her red-knuckled husband. His own drink-gutted father. His uncle pretending he didn't come from where he come from. His needle-bruised brother. The factory jobs that his cousins were so smug and so nervous about that he'd gotten onto just long enough to decide he wanted to get sick of them.

It was all there for her to watch. But she didn't cause it. She fought it. She argued, begged, cussed, threw fits, prayed, studied, and fought over ever one of us, whether we wanted her or not.

And now he wanted nothing to do with them, not even himself. Hadn't she said that anybody that wouldn't stand up wasn't a human but a beast. And who's standin up? *Which one of em aint just layin back and takin it?*

He thought. I don't need to go back. I can just say I never got a ride. Or I got lost. What are they gonna say? Granny aint gonna care. I'm closer to her now than I would be next to that body that aint her body anymore.

And he left the broken side of the barge and walked along it to the shore, the coal and sulphur crackling under his feet, and he looked out across the water. A dim slice of moon lit the watercrests and outlined the Kentucky hills.

He sat in the sand at the water's edge. A train had stalled on the tracks across the river. Its headlamp drew a thin line across the bottom of the hill near the abandoned depot he knew was there, and he wondered what work the people there could be doing.

I don't have to leave here, he thought. I could say I got lost. Or sick.

But that bad taste had never left him. It filled his mouth now and every cell of his tongue was worried with it so that he forgot his hunger and forgot his worry over the funeral and fret and family and he forgot the racket of the crickets.

That taste wasn't only sulphur, though he could smell that all around him. And it wasn't only salt, though that was in it. It was a quivering, fresh split taste, full of iron of the knifeblade, hinting of fester.

104

It was a taste he remembered: Even though he had never put his mouth to it, he remembered it now and tasted it, warm and cold at once, just as he had that day on the street at dusk when the traffic lights are the brightest and you can feel them change and cast the different lights over you even when you can't see them. He had come up to his cousin Darrel, who had jumped up from his stoop to show him, "Look at that, man"—his arm slashed down to the meat, bloodless like a strip of beef in a market, the skin grey as ice around it. He held it out, braced in his left hand like a wounded pet that wanted to break loose. He was reeling: The blacks of his eyes were as big as marbles.

A patrol car slid around the corner, and Darrel saw it. "Hey," he yelled. It stopped. Two cops got out, full of leather like two bulls, and came at him, each from another side so that Lonnie, feeling threatened, backed up to the wall and watched. Each of the cops stood at Darrel's side, but one watched Lonnie and the other spoke, "What's up?"

"Take me up to the hospital man."

The cop said nothing. He began pulling at the pockets of Darrel's army jacket, the four of them, one at a time. When he was done, he motioned Darrel to empty his pants pockets.

"Man I'm hurt. Take me to the hospital." He emptied his left pocket and showed him some change, a package of salted sunflower seeds, a wallet full of cards, and a comb. His right hand wouldn't go in without rasping his wound, so the cop pulled out each pocket for himself: a letter, folded and crumpled, and a handkerchief.

"You been doin pills again," the cop said.
"Why don't you raid 1335 Clay? Those ex-cons are sellin dope. They give it to kids."
"We tried once."
"Take me out to General."

But the cops had already turned back to their car. In a moment, one had written some notes on a pad, the other called in a report over a shoulder radio, and they drove off.

Darrell stood like a shipwreck as the car pulled away. He stood while Lonnie took him by the shoulders and tried to pull him around to sit him back on the stoop. But Darrell shook him off, and went on his own, staring all the while at everywhere but where he was going: at the boards over the windows, at the parking meter head, at the scabs on the knuckles of his left hand.

"What are you doin, man?" Lonnie asked.

"Saginaws." Seconals. Bullet-shaped downers. It could be worse, Lonnie thought. He'd done worse.

A girl was coming down the street. "There's Maggie," Darrel said. She had a pop bottle in her hand. A boy with a twisted leg, his slacks hanging limply around it, stumped beside her.

"Hey, Darrel," he said. "What's happenin?"

Darrel made a motion as if to begin to speak, but he waved the thoughts away, grinning back a laugh and shaking his head as it fell toward his chest. Then he jerked his head back up. "Hey Maggie," he said. Maggie had not looked at him. "Can you get me some stuff?"

She had reached the corner and stood watching the light. Her back was to him. "Yeah," she said. "I can get you some stuff."

"What kind?"

"Speed." She lifted her pop bottle. A car pulled up and slowly rounded the corner as the driver watched her. She turned her head so that she looked at neither the man nor Darrel nor James and drew slowly on the bottle, then brought it down and held it against her hip.

"I don't want speed. I want downs. I'm tryin to kill myself."

"I aint got no downs." She was tired of waiting for the light, and the driver had gone. She looked up the street and stepped off the curb, but a mail truck was coming. She paused, leaning back to look past the mail truck for any other behind him. And as she looked, her brow knit. She said, "What you want to kill yourself for anyway?"

"For three days. I been like this for three days. Aint I James? I aint slept for three days."

The mail truck passed. The WALK light clicked. She started across the street, lifting her pop bottle back to her mouth. James stumped with her; his pants leg flapped like a flag.

Lonnie said, "You better get that arm took care of," thinking, if I can get him to Granny's she'll know what to do for it. Even if the

106

cops won't take him to the hospital.

But Darrel just grinned again, that grin that keeps a laugh from breaking out, and shook his head back down into his chest.

Then the taste came to him. As if someone had forced his mouth down onto the wound, and he could taste in it muscle and fester and blood and even the trace of iron from the blade that had cut him. And with that taste on him, for eight more hours he had worried Darrel over the streets and up to the hospital, arguing with clerks and rent-a-cops, pacing the cigarette-stub corridor, trying to sleep on benches made with arms in the middle to keep people from sleeping, begging for information, hearing Darrel's outraged yell from inside the doctor's room, watching him run out the door and out the room and out the hospital and following him out to the sidewalk where he caught him.

"No way," he said. "I aint lettin that sonofabitch stitch on me." And when he couldn't talk him back in and he couldn't fight him back in, he'd told him to go to hell and he'd gone on home.

And he felt again that worm of guilt. The taste had washed stronger in him.

They found Darrel dead in an alley. The flies were like buttons across the wound.

What Granny'd told him then didn't work. "You did ever thing you could do. You took him as far as you could. They'd already killed him before you got to him is all."

"But I told him myself to go to hell."
"You didn't kill him and you're not to blame. You didn't have no part in it."

But her talking didn't work and he still had let that worm twitch in him and he rambled and complained and blamed until she stuffed her cigarette out in a coffeecup, shook her head, went to the closet, drew back the curtain, and pulled her sewing kit off the shelf. She sat down in her wide-arm chair, pulled her cigarettes out of the kit, tapped a new one out of the pack, put it in her mouth, and balanced it on her lip so that he wondered how she held it on. She rummaged again in the kit for a match, found it, struck it, and lit the cigarette, then squinted her right eye from the smoke, drew deeply, and blew the smoke out across the room. "Boy," she said. "You aint seen nothin out of life yet."

Then she pulled out her quilt top and her needle and thread and began sewing, one crazy patch onto another: triangles, squares, lumps, stars, stop-sign shapes, even circles; picking up with her stitching of ferns and flowers and x-stitches, like the ones that close up a wound.

She wouldn't look at him so he'd gone out onto the street, bought his bullet from Maggie, fired it up, and pumped it into his arm so that he could take it all and rejoice in his grief since the grief was easier to bear than the guilt, and he told his story all over the alleys, telling it as a triumph, as if no one could carry the guilt he carried and live. And as he came down, and it became just plain guilt again it hurt more even than before so he found Maggie again and fired up again and found that time all the ninety-nine things that had to be done and all the people that had to be told and he did them and told them and he rapped and rambled until he started feeling down again and he fired up again and felt his stomach cramp up like a fist and ghosts flew in at the windows that he knew weren't real but he couldn't help fearing until he passed out blank as slate.

When he woke, his throat raw from vomit and from the tube they'd passed into him, it was like floating up from the bottom of a well, and at the top, coming more and more clear, hauling him up, was Granny. He shook his head to clear his eyes. It was her sure enough.

"Had enough?" she asked.

He'd had enough. He stood and listened to the sound of a truck on the highway. Across the river, the train was firing up; its cars were crashing and coupling. He spat the taste of sulphur out of his mouth and started to climb back up the hill.

108

The Road, the River

1.

The river lay smooth and white under the moon as a fresh sheet.
From the window of her trailer, she could see the road, the restaurant to the left with its blue alternating neon sign, river and moon,
and the long spread shanks of the hills. Upriver, to her left, a black
stain soaked down the white sheet, and she saw the slow, blunt
head of a barge with its black rafts of iron behind, pushing down
from the twists of river to the east, reaching for the city. The
barge tugged its members out of the flanks of hills that hid them,
then threw out a long blue leg of light that touched, first, the
Kentucky side, and then her own. The light sifted through the
strip of grey brush on the riverbank, flashed out the concrete of the
docks where they used to bring the coal, ran the yellow timothy
and asphalt and gravel to the restaurant, then for a moment,
crossed her face, brightly blinded her, and filled, like gas explod-
ing into a vacuum, the room behind her. Then just as quickly it
sucked itself back out. The light passed down the shoreline, swung
back to the middle of the river, then drew itself back into the boat.
She could tell the barge then only by its dim red and green running
lights and by its black shape against the white water.

She heard, at a distance, the gaining rush of a car on the
highway. She shut her eyes, heard the sound grow, rush to a
climax, pass, and diminish.

She looked out again. The off-and-on neon was too weak to
reach the barge, too weak to light anything but the restaurant's
door, the gravel of the parking lot, and the grass along its edge.
Off. And on. And again. Some nights they never turned it off even
after closing time, and on those nights the light and its bug-like
electric buzz kept her from her sleep. It could drive her crazy if she
let it.

The barge was out of sight now. Deep along the road, she could
hear the sound of a diesel running at full throttle, and closer, the
sound of the river breaking on the docks. Across the river, under

the black fold of the hills, railroad cars crushed and coupled. She heard a quick scrabble of voices from near the restaurant, and then the neon light went off. The voices carried themselves out of hearing, out to the house behind the restaurant. They left behind them the red firelight from the trash. Then the yard, the restaurant, and her trailer were silent.

She had, this time, slept earlier. Slept, and wakened from a dream so strong she could not yet know if it were dream or memory. She, her uncle, and her older cousin, helping a mare give dry birth in dead winter. The mare had forced out the back legs of her colt, but the body lodged in her flanks, and she had lost her waters and had worn herself to where she no longer gave herself to the pains, but endured them like a beating. Ice lay thin as straw in the trough, and the only light was the yellow oil lantern and the smell of its burning ran syrup through the bowels of the girl and sickened her. She sat on the baled hay with her hands between her knees and watched. Her uncle and her cousin wrapped their hands around the colt's feet, put their boots against the mare's rump, and each time a pain tightened the mare, they pulled the colt a couple more inches out the breach.

They pulled for an hour, and when the colt at last came free, it fell to the floor of the barn like a pile of coiled rope. They looked for the signs, but it had no breath, and the uncle tried first to lift and drop it into shock. But the colt still did not breathe, so he closed the still mouth and one nostril with his hands, put his own mouth over the other nostril, and began to breathe, slow and gentle, into the flat lung of the colt. He pushed into her three times, then laid her back onto the floor of the barn. Just as they gave her up for dead, they saw a shudder of ribs and saw the smoke above her nostrils.

She waited. A rotten, vomity feeling was sliding down her jaws, but she made no move. The diesel had died somewhere, and the railroad cars were silent, but there was the sound of a motor out on the road now. She listened, and it fleshed out and filled the road until, grown into a sound as great as the road could hold, its car sacked into the gravel.

2.

Valery pulled a chair from under the table nearest, dragged it to the door, set it under the big fan over the door, stepped up onto the chair with a punctured breath, reached up, pulled the plug from the socket at the side of the fan, then heard the fan's snarl break sharply, saw the blades go grey and sort themselves out, and heard the fan whoop slowly whoop into silence.

Andy was in the back. He'd finished the mopping, and she could hear him kicking the buckets into the closet. She stepped down from the fan, nudged the chair back under its table, straightened a span of menus, turned, and walked behind the counter. "You got it clean in there?" she hollered.

"What?" The closet door kicked closed, and the light from the room back of the kitchen went off.
"I said, you got it clean in there?"
"I been cleanin aint I?"

You aint never gonna get a straight answer from him, she thought. You ought to know after these nineteen years you aint never gonna get a straight answer from him. "Well come on," she said, "let's get out of here." She got an itch, each night at this time, to get out of there. She got like an animal in a bag; she felt the place begin to choke her. Two garbage sacks waited on the floor. She picked up the one nearest and started toward the door. Sweet rotting fruit and grease ran through the nostrils and into her gut, and for a moment, she clutched. She set the bag down by the door, pulled her jacket from off the metal rack and slipped it on, thinking, He'll find something more to dawdle on. He was whistling something tuneless and broken. She grimaced, and felt the slack place in her cheek made when she lost the teeth on her whole left side of her face the time the brick hit her. Let him take his damn good time, she thought. He always does anyway. "Don't forget the garbage," she yelled back at him. Then she picked the garbage sack back up and stepped out the door.

There was a small wind off the river, and she pulled her jacket closer. It's cool now, she thought. It'll warm up in the day. That's the way fall weather is. She could feel the coming fog in the air, even though she could see no trace of it on the river or on the hills. It'll roll in about the time that boy's rollin out, she thought, taking the thought back soon as she made it. She looked over to the trailer

111

they'd given the girl. There was no light, no car. Maybe he's not comin this night, she thought. He came most nights. On her free nights, he took the girl out. Other nights, he stayed some hours, and left. There'll be a night he leaves and don't come around again at all, she thought. Then she'll see how it ought to be. She caught this thought back as well, thinking, There aint no harm in the girl; she's just wild.

She was walking slowly, holding the garbage slung in both hands and balanced on her hip. The gravel hurt right through her shoes. Over by the trash barrel, near the edge of the band of light made and unmade as the neon flared and retreated, a pair of yellow animal eyes lit and unlit with each alteration of the sign. Another goddam coon, she thought. "Git," she shouted, but the eyes made no move. She stooped, picked up a stone, and without rising from her crouch, flung and shouted, "Git, goddamn it," and the eyes disappeared.

"Did you git him?" Andy was at the door, holding the keys in his hand.

"It wouldn't hurt him if I did," she said. He never could find the right key. "Don't forget the lights," she said. "It keeps the girl from her sleep." He reopened the door, reached in, groped for the switch, found it, and the yard went dark for a moment until their eyes learned to use the moonlight.

"It aint them lights that keeps that girl from her sleep," he said, pitching himself down the stairs in the motion that was almost like falling: Each night, coming down those stairs, his body slung forward and collapsed like a puppet whose strings are suddenly cut. And yet each time, at the fifth and bottom step, he seemed to swing a third hand out behind him to grab the strings together and jerk himself back up. Sometimes he's not gonna make that catch, she thought, and I'm gonna have to pick him up and haul him away like a sack of potatoes.

She's got more'n that light to keep her from her sleep," he repeated. "That boy keeps her from more sleep than a hundred of them lights."

"You hesh," she said. "For one, it aint half true. For another, it aint your business if it is." The girl always did her work, as well as any, better than most. That was what they paid her for. She had the morning shift, most days, the breakfasts for the truckers and the rivermen. Valery and Andy paid her and they let her keep the trailer. "At least she don't sell it, like some we've had in that trailer." And even if she did, she thought, it would still be her own affair. As long as those girls did their work and went honest, Valery never cared what they did on their own time. It wasn't her place to think on it.

A dog, one of the dogs from up the hollar, flung up a long, singing, watery, winding yell up in the hill. The yell broke, then twisted up high and thin for a moment more, then broke, rose briefly once more, and again, and then the dog was silent. Girls came down out of those hills hungry and wild: not mean, and not even foolish, but hungry, so you couldn't tell them a thing.

Andy was whistling again, slowly and tunelessly, but now it didn't jar her. It was different: It was empty as water. They said nothing. She felt no urgency now that there was no longer the restaurant to scramble out of, so she let herself feel tired. She walked just quickly enough to let the garbage smell pass behind her. The air was cool, but not sharp. The hint of fog softened it, and she could sleep well; they could sleep late.

The small breeze cupped into the hollow of the firewall rattled the ashes from the night before. The fires never burned the things clear down the way they should, and that was what drew the coon and possum down from the hollar. She could smell the river with its hint of fog, then the rancid ashes, then both together. The wire basket stood out against the firewall like the dark trees against the darker hills. She dropped her bag into the basket, then waited for Andy. He dropped his in after, fumbled through three different pockets, found his matches, knelt, struck, and let the small flame catch the paper of Valery's sack. The flame found the grease and ragged out quickly over the whole of both sacks, and peeling the brown paper away, licked over milk cartons, potato peels, fish heads, scraps of bread, chicken bones, eggshells, meat wrappings, pie crusts, butter papers. A trick of wind brought the smoke into her face and reached for her throat. She coughed once and turned away. That part of the day was over. She looked out to the river to see if the fog had started to roll up. The moon was higher over the water, but there was no trace of the mist that she felt coming. "The fire'll take care of itself," she said to him. "It's late." The smell was clean and smoky. They could sleep well; they could sleep late.

She had just let herself settle into the bed when she heard the car pull in at the girl's trailer. He oughtn't to come in now, she thought. It aint but a few hours til she's supposed to get up. Andy looked out the window and recognized the car, but Valery didn't stay awake long enough to find out if the boy stayed or left.

113

3.

Her face was white in the window when he slung the car around in the yard. The headlights banked off the white siding of the restaurant, slashed across the whole front of the trailer, and caught her face in the window, her hands on the windowframe. She ducked back quick. When he hit the brakes, spun the rear end to the right, and collared the car to a stop, he thought he would see her at the door. He cut the engine and the lights, and the car shuddered silent, and he felt woods and darkness, river and silence swim at him suddenly and swamp him, and his brain and butt spun with the arrested motion like two pinwheels, one at each end of a stick. He waited until he could climb above the spinning, the reached around into the back seat for one of the bottles, twisted the cap off, rolled down the window, tossed out the little pan of metal, took a long pull that cleared the neck of the bottle, and waited for her to show at the door. He didn't even feel the beer go down. He'd been drinking all that night, and he always stopped tasting them or even really knowing them from water after he first felt the bottom of his brain erase itself and felt the top of his brain wheel like a buzzard through the empty spaces of his skull.

But he was feeling good. He'd just made it thirty miles in twenty minutes over roads twisted like a dog's back leg. He'd made it with half a case of beer in his gut and a back seat full of six packs. It was pay night, and he was letting everybody know. And everybody knew in the half dozen bars he'd sat in up and down the curve of river before he remembered he should have been seeing her. "A three hundred and sixty-five horsepower engine," he'd been saying. He'd rebuilt it himself: polished the parts like plate and fitted them like clockwork. "Dual carburetors, headers, mag wheels, dual exhaust, racing stripes cross the top, tach, four-speed heavy-duty transmission, and a leather interior." Then he remembered. Oh hell she'll be mad, he thought. He stopped talking, slapped his money down on the bar, picked up his sixpacks, threw them into the car, jumped on the accelerator, and flung the car all up and down the road. He slid, skidded, fishtailed, and flew around more curves than he wanted to count, letting the carburetors open up like oven doors and feeling each rod kick like a cow's leg. It was a car that could take it. Now, stopped, he could feel the heat leaving the motor and he heard the quiet smack of oil running back into the pan.

The spinning all up and down his spine slowed and he looked again toward the trailer door. He could see the screen but nothing behind it, so he opened the car door, reached out a foot to find solid ground, then pivoted himself up like the arm of a clock and stood leaning against the fender, trying to find his legs and trying to see his way through the screen. The jellied nerves of his legs restrung themselves, but the screen refused him. I can't even see if the door's open, he thought. He stood a moment more but heard nothing, thinking, She'd say something if she was there so maybe she aint there. Then, But maybe she's there and she's mad so she don't want to talk. "Darlene," he yelled, "Come on out here. I got something to tell you." The screen door had no voice, and nothing behind it moved, so he staggered across the yard finding more of himself as he moved, and coming to the door, he ducked, ran his face against the screen, peered, saw nothing, and stood again. Nothing was darker than the darkness of that screen. Damn, he thought, she didn't even come to the door when she seen me. He swung an arm around, found the door, and pounded. "Darlene," he shouted. "Come on out here. I got to talk to you."

He could hear her move in the trailer. There was no way a person could move in that small rattly trailer without making some kind of sound. He knew that. "Come on out." He caught the note of pleading in his own voice and stopped himself. Now dammit, he thought, I come all this way. He thumped the door again, only this time he didn't hear her move. He knocked until the hinges started loose from their hold, and when he heard behind his pounding the sound of her steps, he stopped. Her pull broke the air seals around the door, and he could see her with her hair down across her shoulder, her face placid as stone. "Now what do you want," she said.

"I don't want *not* in," he said. "How come you wouldn't open that door?"

"I don't feel right. Go on home."

"I come here to talk to you."

"You talk some other time. I don't feel right."

"I just drove..."

"Go on home. It's late. I don't feel right. Go on home."

She shut the door. He didn't hear her move away for a minute or so, and he tried to figure out what to do. On another night he would have started to pound on the door again, and he knew that if he wanted to, he could break the door in half. But he held himself

115

back. There was something in her voice that scared him now to think about it, and he was too drunk to figure out whether he wanted to handle it or not. He heard her slip down the length of the trailer to the bedroom, then he sat down on the step of the trailer, put his elbows on his knees, and raced his fingers through his hair to try to stop the numbness crawling like a snake around his scalp. He gave it up when the numbness had him circled. Then he stood, caught himself when his upward motion swung him too far forward and the shifting blood brought shock back to his brain. Then he took the unsure, treacherous steps back to the car.

The numbness slipped away when he moved. He leaned against the car door and looked back at the trailer. She had him too scared to think anything straight and half a dozen notions ran through him before he thought, She aint been right, not for a week. He didn't want that. There was something dangerous in such a thought. Goddam women, he thought. They all get like that. This thought was safe enough for him, and he started to leave. He opened the car door, caught glint of the foil on the sixpacks, thought What the hell, and lifted one of the sixpacks out of the back, pulled himself up from the carseat, shut the door, and headed off toward the clear placed he knew on the side of the hill, past the trailer, out where the hill watched out on the river.

The weeds slashed his legs with dew when he broke through them. He remembered to duck the low branches of the short, wildly broad persimmon tree by the path, and as he bent, he kicked one of the small fallen persimmons into the brush. He threaded himself and the sixpack through the net of sapling branches that reached across the path, then he stopped and looked around him. The white moon hung low in the stripped branches of the persimmon tree like a drunk woman on a corncrib roof laughing down at him.

He sat, pulled the first beer out of the carton, shivered once, and twisted off the cap. He dropped the cap beside him, then pulled at the beer until he lost his breath. The beer hit him quickly, shook off the last coil of numbness, and set his brain running again. He was at that point where the bottom of his brain was erased beyond numbness and the top of his brain was moving, buzzard-slow and tighteningly circular, cutting down to a point that he could not yet see, that lay in some thicket of his mind like a dead rabbit.

He held the beer cupped in his hands, and he listened. There were sounds far out on the highway, but the railroad cars on the

Kentucky side were silent. The river, behind the fracturing black of the trees below him, was white and empty. Some small animal, a coon or possum, racketed in the brush somewhere off to his right, and he tensed for a moment out of an ancient fear of night sounds. But nothing came out of the brush. It was too late in the year for snakes; he could be easy. He heard dogs yelling somewhere up in the hills, but they cried only when they found a track. He heard the timed, low, evasive haunt of an owl and the tick of the black leaves rotting into the ground.

He finished the second beer, pulled out a new one, and opened it. He drank more slowly this time, but he pulled for just as long, and when he took the bottle away, he set it on the ground between his feet with the beer dancing up the sides of the bottle. He could see a dim hint of road through the trees, and farther upstream where the trees and brush had all been cut away from the riverbank, he could just make out the dock. They'd drunk wine and done fine things down by that dock, back in the summer, back before the girl got strange. The moon excited the rising mist into a white brew that broke up the darkness...but it was dense like milk. There were only the black weave of trees, the scraps of pavement and dock, the moon, and the white river. The sound of a truck was building off to the right, coming from the city. He could tell about where it was by the depth of the sound and by the way the throttle narrowed for the curves and opened for the straightaways. Damn truckers, he thought. They're the ones that gets the ass.

He arched his arm back with the empty bottle till his fingers touched the cold grass behind him and flung it, with a wrench that hurt his stomach muscles, down the hill toward the road. The bottle fell short somewhere in the brush, bobbled a couple times more, then whispered to a stop in the grass. He shrugged.

The truck was closer now: He could hear the shifts the driver made for the last pair of curves and the sound grew larger, built like floodwaters behind a wall, then broke from behind the hill as the truck took the last bend. He saw the lights flash first into the milk over the river then turn onto the road. A short twist in the road brought it into the thicket below him for a moment, then passed it back again. Light and sound grew thicker and heavier until the truck broke across the open strip of highway below him, ripped out its peak sound, left a flash of taillight, and was gone.

The next beer was warmer when he pulled it out. Those damn truckers is the ones, he thought. I ought to get me a job as a trucker.

117

He was working as a logger now, and sometimes he ran the truck into town with the logs for the mill. But it wasn't anything like what the truckers got. It wasn't bad. There were snakes in the woods, and the work was heavy, but they didn't always work. So it wasn't bad. But it wasn't anything like what the truckers got. They got all they wanted. He looked down the hill to the house, the restaurant, and the trailer. The top of his brain was still spinning, like the buzzard, but more this time like something trapped in ellipsis, a satellite, rocking pole to pole with no way to find center. He opened the beer and drank, trying to pull himself off the track and down to where he could stop.

The spinning slowed in his skull, but only because his brain felt heavier and spun still more fixedly in place. He remembered: He'd been whirling drunk in the trailer and reached after her and banged his elbow on a cabinet. She laughed and he turned with his arm still too dazed to pull his hand into a fist, and turning, he found her where he had not thought to find her and they found their way among bureaus and shelves and over chairs and footstools and she pulled him slowly down. He was half-helpless with his still-dazed arm and he felt the silent jerking hilarity of her laugh beneath him. Then the laughing stopped. *No*, she said. *Let me do it.*

That was the first he had of her, and he had what he'd wanted of her. But he had not gotten what he had not known he wanted. She had rutted him onto the track.

House, restaurant, and trailer were still. The moon was picking its way through its black net of branches. Sometime before morning the mist would blind the white houselights hung in the hills on the Kentucky side. He wanted to blind himself and sleep.

She's probably knocked up, he thought. That's how they get. They get sick like that. The last beer had left a taste of iron in his mouth. If she's knocked up, I guess it's me, he thought. But if it's me, she ought to tell me. I could do something if she told me. He sat on the thought. The hill was getting cold, and he shivered. Maybe she don't even know, he thought. She hadn't said anything, not that night nor any night before that. But she'd know, he thought. She'd know and not tell me at all. That's her way. He'd told her: You get in trouble and I'll do what's right, and she'd said: I get in trouble, I'll find my own way out. I won't need you.

And that was what galled. He had nothing in it but a quick

118

splurge of birthmilk. His pride was cut. She don't want a damn thing out of me, he thought. He felt ghostly, useless, improbable as mist, dead as leaves.

Another racket broke into the thicket to the right, and he heard a heavy dogtread snapping the leaves and a sharp hunting snuff in the dirt. The dog sensed him, stopped, set up a low growl, and crouched. He saw the two dim bulbs of the dog's eyes dip suspiciously, then rise. "Whoa dog," he said. The growl stopped. "Come on," he said, and a big-boned plot, mottled like a copperhead, plodded out of the black brush and into the cleared circle of grass and light. His haunches dropped, and a back leg lifted, touched tentatively twice behind an ear, found the spot that bothered him, then pumped a half dozen times in a precise and well-oiled motion. "What you been up to dog?" he asked. The dog dropped his front legs, yawned, then lowered his muzzle across his crossed paws; his eyes drifted shut a moment, then raised themselves, then found a place where they could rest and watch at the same time. The two, man and dog, sat together as the moon took itself branch by branch out of the persimmon tree and pitched itself westward toward the city. The man nursed down the last half of his beer and placed the bottle at his side. The dog rested and watched until another hound's yell ran down to them from somewhere up in the hill. The dog jumped up, barked once at the call, then followed it into the brush.

The man waited until he could no longer hear the rattle and slip of the dog through the leaves and briars, then he stood. I'm too drunk to stay here, he decided and he stretched the stiffness out of his back and legs and waited until the spinning of his brain slowed enough that he could master himself. Then he began to take himself in careful drunken steps down the hill. In the wet grass, the weak bodies of the fallen persimmons slipped like human flesh under his feet.

4.

The first pain come on her after she heard him pull away. She stood by the window again, waiting. And when the first pain came on her she clutched and started thinking quick as water, I aint gonna get caught. I aint gonna get caught. Even if it kills me, I aint gonna get caught. She kept up thinking all through the first pain, even as it ripped her down like a knife fighting jungles through her bowels, I aint gonna get caught. The pain turned tight and heavy as rock and dropped her to the bed, and she lay buckled like a broken weed, her legs pushed up against her breasts as if she thought she could crush the pain out of her and be rid of it. But the pain fought her; it clawed at all her insides and held. She had to take it till she lost all track of time. Then it retreated and hid in some hollow of her body and she washed into a blood-black sleep.

She had not slept since she'd wakened from her dream, not all that time since the boy had pounded on the door. It wasn't that he was drunk, nor that she feared him. He'd been drunk before, and once, he'd slapped her up and down the trailer. But it wasn't that. This time it was the waiting. She found a thousand sounds in the trailer; she found a thousand movements in her body. But none of them was what she waited for, and she waited as a person waits under an axe. The boy had come, late, just as she'd thought he would, and she'd told him to go, just as she would have any time he would have come that night. He was easily told. The pain would not be told. It had come finally out of hiding, had torn at her, and worn her out. So she slept.

The boy stirred in her new dream, and she woke angry, sick, and afraid. Hell with him, she thought. Her dream was blank, but for the dim stir of the boy and but for one notion: I thought I was dead. Some part of me thought the rest of me was dead or that all of me was dead and I was being thought by somebody else.

She was still doubled over, and she shivered all through the twists of her shoulders, back, and legs. She feared this chill even more than the pain, so she tried to pull the sheets and blankets up over herself. But her fingers refused to pull together, and a weak, tentative, silly raggedness ran through her body. This angered her more and scared her more, and she gave up the blankets and lay like a broken weed at the bottom of a creek and tried to force her inert and insubordinate muscles, nerves, bones, and tendons to work themselves together and she grew more angry and more

120

scared until her anger and fear forced her loose and she sat up on the bed. Her head felt clouded and crazy as if it had been blown full of milkweed. But she waited, more patiently this time, and the craziness passed.

By the time she stood, all feeling had lifted like mist. She was turned to quartz, and moving, felt no movement in her limbs. Her clock glowed like Jesus on the table; it was four hours until she was to open up the restaurant for the truckers and the men who ran down to work in the city. Out her window, the moon had curded the mist. But that was unimportant now. She had turned to quartz, and nothing could break through her. From where she stood, she could touch almost anything in the room. She leaned against the table that held her mirror and felt the darkness pass into her, into every seam of the stone of her, down to the small red cloud that threaded through her center. The cloud was dark already, so the darkness could not touch it. She felt safe, all untouchable stone and darkness. So she felt cheated when the pain, stonehard against the ball of mere muscle, bone, and membrane in her belly, kicked out again. It pulled at her as if it had found a hitch to a truck, and she buckled, caught the dresser, and swung by it back to the table. The weight of stoneheavy pain almost dropped her to the floor, but she held onto the wood, and pushed with both hands, hoping to push so hard she could knock herself out or force the pain to drop out of her. But her brain began to drift, and she felt her hold go loose. So she carried the pain to the bed and let it throw her down. Oh God, she thought. It can't be too many more of these. It can't be.

It looked like a fish. The ball of sponge and blood had broken open as it came out of her, and in the lamplight she could see the light curled figure, no bigger than a minnow. Pity eddied in the hollows where the pain had hidden. She had little time. The bed was full of her blood, and she was weak from the pain, but she knew she could have no rest.

Three times she had been twisted and the thing had cut its way out of her. And now she had rested briefly, had stopped her blood, and had washed herself, and she was packing, slowly. She was weaker than she thought she could be without being unable to move. The blood had left her light-headed, and her fingers still would not close tight, but she was able to pick up her things and drop them into the bag. If I can just keep moving, she thought, I won't pass out. I'll get my strength back when I can rest.

She sat the bag down near the door, and turned to the bed. She didn't look this time; the blood was beginning to stink like wet newsprint. She tugged at the sheets until they gave, wrapped them all around the patch of nearly dried blood and soggy flesh, and limped with the bundle to the door. She could walk, but when she walked, someone set hooks on her insides and tried to drag them out. She could only stop the tearing at her wound if she walked with her legs pressed close together as if she were trying to hold a stick between them. At the door, she stopped. I better leave a note, she thought. So she put the bundle down beside her bag, walked her hurts back to the table, found a pencil and a piece of paper, and wrote,

Nobody killed me. I just left.

She signed it, walked back to the door, flipped off the light picked up her bundle and her bag, and stepped, slowly so that she would not tear the wound, outside.

She looked over to the trash burner once. I could throw it there she thought. I could throw it in the woods. She looked down at the white and black, strangely heavy bundle in her hands, bit her lip, thought, It aint garbage, then headed across the gravel of the yard toward the road and the river. She listened as she walked. I won't be fast enough to get out of the way if somethin's comin, she thought. There was no sound on the road, so she set the bag down and pulled herself over the asphalt, across the berm, through the wet timothy, and down the grade that led to the dock. There was a small muddy depression, a fontanelle, at the bottom of the slope, just in front of the dock; its water gripped at her ankles and soaked through the canvas of her shoes. In drier ground near the dock, she looked for a stone. The moon had passed, and the sun was only cracking the shamble of fog as it rolled off the river. So she stopped, felt through the wet grass, pulled a rock bigger than her hand from the mud, then stood. She stepped onto the concrete dock and walked with the rock and the bundle toward the water. She could feel the small chunks of coal break between her feet and the concrete, but she could not see the edge of the dock. Her head was getting lighter. I could fall in, she thought. I could fall in and drown cold without the strength even to move a hand. So she slowed her step. When she saw among the coal bits the iron lip of the dock, she stopped, opened the bundle, slipped in the stone, rewrapped it, then dropped the whole thing into the water. She could tell by the broad muffled splash the bundle made that it had not lost the rock. She didn't bother to watch it sink. She closed her eyes, hunched her shoulders, and rubbed each arm with her hands. Her jacket was cold and wet with mist, and some stranger wetness hinted itself along her legs. I got to move, she thought. I'll die out here on this dock if I don't get movin. She almost had to crawl to get back up the hill.

By the time the sun was a white disk high behind the wall of mist, she was on the road to the city with her bag, hurting, holding her wound shut, waiting for her strength, hoping for a ride.

The Knot

1. Earl

He was trying to re-tie the knot. He wanted to be sure. The moon, the first dim witness, had started up over the wall. In just a short time, just when the moon peaked over the courtyard, over the rehab's fire escape where he worked, surrounded, between the empty house and the one they were rebuilding, he would be ready. No mistakes.

From the empty house, he smelled wine, mold, urine. From the rehab, he smelled sawdust, new concrete, plaster. He took the smells deep into his nostrils, thinking, This'll be a good house for somebody someday. But it sure wasn't for us.

To work, he had some light from the growing round pate of the moon, and he had some from the street, for the lamp light passed through the hallway and filled the floor of the court and glanced up to the fire escape. Light running down and light glancing up. Sky light and streetlight. He was balanced between them, working at his knot.

It was the third time he had reworked it. First he had tied it to the stairs. But when he had stepped out on them, the stairs tilted downward under his weight. *That aint no good*, he thought. *My feet'll touch the ground.* So he tried to tie it to the bar that held the counterweight. But then he had looped it through the stairs so that the belt wasn't long enough to let him get off. He thought, *I'll get tangled in the iron.* So he figured it out. He passed it round-armed to the side of the stairs and then reached through the stairs with his other hand to reach it to the bar where he could tie it. It was hard to stretch out there for the work, but that was the way to do it. No mistake.

The rabbit goes up the hole, around the tree, and back down in the hole. Pull.

It had been nearly as hard on the other end. The buckle was cold when he belted his neck, and it nestled cold as a wellstone against the place where his jaw notched in and it pressed on his glands and gristles and it made his mouth water with a taste like nails and the

124

strangeness of it made him crazy to be done with the work and so he moved the buckle around to the front of his neck. But then it pressed on his Adam's apple like a nutcracker and he could feel every beat of his blood in it and that beating, like it was a snake at his throat, was all he could think of. So he jerked it loose to free himself from all that beating and when he was calmed down enough he put it at the back of his neck, in the little hollow where his brain set into his spine. It didn't feel right there either—the buckle scraped at the lumps in his skull. But it was the best he had.

So that had made one end tight. And now he was stretching out his hands with the other end to the weight and working on his knot. And once he had both ends fast, he'd be ready.

The rabbit goes up the hole. Around the tree. Back down in the hole.

2. John

The first he knew of it was his mother running up the street at him with her eyes wide and wild in the way that he knew: Somebody's died. And behind her were fuzz-headed Lloyd and William and LittleJack and that colored boy Lonnie that hung with them, all stalking behind her without needing to rush because she couldn't run fast. But they all had their faces set hard and their hands all fisted up so that he knew: There's been trouble and somebody's died. From around the corner and down the block, red lights flickered and flared. He set his suitcase down on the sidewalk and walked into the street just as she was turning the corner. She saw him then and stopped like she thought he was the one who was dead and she looked at him like she couldn't tell for sure.

She put her hand against the light pole for balance and said in a lost voice that was breathless from running, "You're back." It was like she was sorry she couldn't be better to him for just coming home from such a long homeless trip. She looked down the street and a red flood now filled and emptied her stony face. John looked down the block and saw the spinning red lights from the police cars and the life squad. And she said, as the lights filled and unfilled her face, and a roar of staring people rose at him from down the street, "Earl's done hung hisself. Just now."

A cry chipped in her throat like a bird in a shell and she might have screamed it out, but William said, "Let's go, Ma," and she went off with the stalking boys like the stone on a drag, down the street into the milling lights and people.

Up at the house he could see Jack. He was leaning in the doorframe with the babies holding his legs. He was nodding at some man in the street and grinning.

That bastard. That grin. I can bet what he's sayin: One damn thing after another.

He don't have to talk like that. Earl aint his son, but he aint no stranger either. He aint my full brother either, but he's brother enough. Aint? Wasn't. She said he's hung hisself. Hung hisself. They just think that cause somebody told them that. He surely aint hung hisself. That's a fact. He wouldn't know how. That's a fact. There aint no way.

He started to follow them, but his shin caught on the bare metal corner of the suitcase and scuffed it into the gutter and he thought, *I could just pick up this damn thing and get on out of here and miss all of this. That's what I need to do.*

Then he could be out on his road again, away from the television and wailing and Jack's sneer and the babies that ran into the walls and cried.

But an anger and a dread opened up in him like a pit of snakes in the Spring, and he thought, *Earl aint hung hisself. That's sure. Somebody done it to him.* And he thought, Aint nobody gonna do a thing about it either. Not Jack. He won't even want to bury him right cause it'll be too much money. And not them police. They're just as glad he's dead. It's just us.

And he forgot the suitcase and followed them down the long block to where the police stood at the hallway door of the place where they all lived back when he first had found them all. Where he and those other boys had spread themselves to the basement to sleep in midwinter as they collected themselves: John, William, Lloyd, and Earl from their travels and adoptions, the babies back from the Home after Jack started getting his check, the colored boy Lonnie when he started hanging around, Little Jack that was one of Jack's kids by somebody else. It was a place where the rats jumped over the table just a hair faster than somebody could throw a shoe. Where the police car slowed down to watch them and listen to the squawk of its radio as it passed each night. Where Jack traded cars, six at a time and they filled the street with the jacked up cars and pools of oil. Where they'd fought the boys from the corner every night because they laughed at their clothes and because they'd try to raise Earl into a fit. Where they got finally kicked out for their shotguns and garbage, for pissing in the courtyard, for their nine dogs, and for not paying the rent.

When John caught up with them at the edge of the ring of watchers, he could see police at their cars, at the door of the courtyard, and milling through the upstairs rooms, their white hats wheeling and bobbing in the light like pond ducks.

Ma didn't even try to break past the cop who stopped her at the door. John had followed her and the boys as they broke into the crowd of maybe thirty people as she screamed, "Where is he? I want to see him. I got to see him. I got a right to see him." And she bulled her way through the people who leaned together two by two and who pointed to the house, the police, and the hallway door. One man, unseeing, stepped into her way and she knocked into his shoulder and without even looking at him swung her arm wide at him and would have hit him open-handed if William hadn't grabbed the man from behind and jerked him by the shoulders back so that he and Lloyd could twist up his arms and hold him from swinging back at her if he had a mind to.

She forgot her swing and stumbled for her balance as she drove on toward the door. John came up behind her just before she stopped, ignoring the cop at the door at the top of the steps who was saying what she already wasn't bothering to hear about not passing the hallway door because what she saw was not the cop but, through the hall and behind the cop, the shoulders, back, and clawed-up hands of dead strung-up Earl.

His head and whatever cord held him up there were blocked by the hallway ceiling. But that was him. There was no mistake. That was Earl's boat-shaped back, and the hands that had strangely reached themselves upward and frozen behind his back were Earl's stumpy, peg-fingered hands. In the light from the street, Earl's hands were blue like bruises, and even through the netting of grease that lay always in the creases of his skin, John could see in the center of the back of Earl's right hand the black-furred-over mole that swallowed light like a well.

Like distant lightning, a camera flashed against him.

She had stopped even before the cop had put one hand on each end of his stick and held the stick crosswise in front of his chest like a gate. She put her fingers to her mouth and said, automatically, as a protest that she no longer cared to make or leave unmade, "Not even to see my own boy."

John could see him too, and the other boys could see him as they crowded over John's shoulders. And it was Earl. No mistake. There was nobody else built like that, with such ham-shaped legs with the pants cuffs turned up three times to fit and the belt line way up at his rib cage, and such a keel-sharp spine that sloped his shoulders forward even now while his head was strung straight up, with such stubby hands that now were so strangely leafed up even though he was surely too dead to hold them up himself.

John looked over to his mother. She saw, he knew, the mole, the hands, the ham-hock legs, the rowboat spine. Her fingers rubbed over her mouth. She said, 'For all that hurtin, this is what it all come to."

By the growing shadow that Earl's frozen hands made against his back, John could tell that, slow as a clock, Earl was turning.

●

Like a monkey. That's how they left him, John thought later. *They wouldn't cut him down nor untie him either. Not for an hour. Cause they had to get their pictures. And the reporters had to come for theirs. And they had to write down everything about everything that was there. So we had to stand there on the street watching him strung up there like a monkey on that belt.*

He might have lived if they'd taken him down off there soon enough. They found him a half hour before we even got there. It might have been time enough. But they didn't want him to live.

And once they took him down off there they never even took the belt off his neck.

The men had come in from the Workhouse bodies detail and while one stood on the fire escape and unworked the belt, two others, under guard, stood on garbage cans and lifted Earl on their shoulders to give him slack.

When he was loose and they brought him down to put him in the plastic bag, all those on the street saw his face, pale as seed, for the first time. His mouth was open, round as a howl, and his lips and cheeks were blue-black like a possum's gums. His eyes were closed: more than closed: clenched.

John thought, *He's choked to death. It never broke his neck. If he'd broke his neck he'd never have turned blue that way. He died chokin on that belt. And that's why his hands is clawed up that backwards way.*

When the Workhouse prisoners finally brought bagged-up Earl on a stretcher toward the car the cop with the crossways-held stick shoved them back to the street. And while Ma was being pushed one way she was being called another because enough people had pointed her out that the police had finally called her over and asked her questions that she answered with just a few words at a time and without ever looking at the cop and his clipboard but always at Earl until they had him loaded, had the doors shut, had the workhouse men locked back in their car, and had Earl started off toward the morgue. As soon as Earl's car was just out of sight around a corner she never answered another question that the man asked, even though he asked five times more until some neighbor finally said to him, "You know she just lost a son." The cop shook his head and let her alone.

John had been watching Earl's slow spin on the belt, and when he turned, he saw Ma had been separated from him and the rest. *And she's lookin around and seein nothin but strangers and some of em cops and it'll break her for sure.* Her wall—*she's built this wall like stone around her so she'll not feel the whole thing all at once and break down in the street*—had started to break down. Her eyes shot like lizards through the people and when she couldn't see any of them, her eyes went empty and her jaw dropped open under the force of a cry trying to force its way out. *Once she's ready*, he thought, *She'll dance and call on Jesus and cuss Jack and hug on the babies, all at once. But she's not ready for that yet.* So he yelled out, "We're back here," and she heard him and she started to come back to them.

●

"Come with us," the one with the clipboard said to Ma close to his car. When he looked around, all of them, Mae, John, Lloyd, Black Lonnie, and Little Jack, stood together at the car door and he said, "Look, I'll take three of you." And John said, "You got room. We'll all go." And he grabbed the back door handle and let his mother into the seat and the others ran around the car for places and the cop shrugged, sat at the wheel, stowed his clipboard beside his seat, and drove them off. John thought, *You can't hardly get them to carry you to a hospital, but they'll pack you off to this dead house.*

William, Lloyd, and Lonnie sat with their faces full of stones and fury. But Little Jack, in his seat next to the cop, his feet on the hump and his knees in his face, pondered the dials and switches of the dashboard, the papers of the clipboard, and the belt of leather and lead.

At the morgue, the white-coated men wheeled Earl out on a tray, unzipped the bag, and pulled back the sheet over him to show his face so she could tell it was really him that was dead. He was naked, pale as putty. They had taken off the belt, and his neck was a brown spoil of veins where the belt had bruised him. His tongue bulged under the blue of his lips. John looked for his hands, for the hooked-up fingers and gristles and the black of his mole, but they only took the sheet down past his shoulders.

She said, "That's Earl. That's my boy." And one man went for new papers for her to sign to say that was Earl and to say they could cut on him to take him apart to tell the cause of his death. And John thought, *I could tell them the cause of his death real quick and they wouldn't even need to touch him. He hung off that rehab house with that belt around his neck so it choked off his windpipe and his tongue filled up his mouth and he couldn't breathe no more. They don't need to cut on him. They just want to practice.*

The other man zipped up Earl's bag and started to wheel him through a door, into a room, up to a wall full of cabinets. Then the door swung closed behind him. John thought, *If they've taken that belt off of him, they must have it somewhere. To keep for evidence. I'd like to see that belt sometime. Just to see. I'd like to see the knot he tied.*

Them men want to cut him up and pass chemicals through him to see did he do it himself and did he have drugs in him and then say what they think about it. But Ma aint lettin em. Them boys think somebody else done it to Earl and they got their ideas. And them cops got their ideas. But Ma don't want none of them to fool with Earl. She just wants to get him put into the ground and let him rest.

But still I'd like to see that knot he tied. From what I seen of that knot, Earl could of never tied it. But I guess even Earl could do something when he tried long enough. So I reckon he could have

130

made that knot.

Still, I'd like to of seen that knot. I'd like to know how it was done. I'd like to know how ever bit of it was done.

3. Earl

He entered, and the darkness swamped him, lipped him over, filled him, and sunk him, like water into a well-bucket. Thin cords of light ran along the sides of the hall, past him toward the court. But what he felt and what was drowning him was the darkness, for treading that darkness, he felt he was all of a sudden in no place at all, and being in no place he carried himself into places he was not ready to go back to: cabins and highways, caves and alleys. And if he let all that drown him he would never make it up the stairs. So he reached out a hand, touched the wall along one of the thin cords of light, and felt the rough surface of the bricks.

This is how I'll have to go, he thought. And he handed himself along the wall til the wall ended and the cord of light ran out and he was in the middle of the court with no moonlight yet and the loose cords of streetlight too dim to see anything but the line where the bricks of the wall met the cement floor of the court, the shadow ironwork of the fire escape, and the dark line of the rooftops that surrounded him.

The door's over here to the left somewhere, he remembered. He reached out through the swimming dark for the wall, took the two steps he knew he had to take, then touched the bricks and felt along them until he touched the upright metal bar of the doorframe, then felt the cold blind draft of the hall.

They aint put in the door yet, he reckoned. He reached his hand inside for the wall, stepped in, and felt his way along the wall to the corner. It was a new drywall. He could feel the close grain of the paper sheeted over the wallboard, and in the corner, the cool grain of the spackling.

Now the stairs is just a few steps over. He walked three more blind steps, found the first stair step, then started up, one at a time, balancing himself by his right hand on the wall, feeling for each step because he had not yet gauged the height and he wasn't sure anymore how many there were. He knew the house from when they'd lived there before.

131

But you don't remember everything. He stopped where he thought it might be halfway and took his hand away from the wall. The first thing he felt was the pure submerging darkness. Then the silence that drummed over his ears.

This is almost what it'd be like, he thought. *If I could just stay here like this I wouldn't need to do all that work. But it aint that easy.*

God I hear. He heard voices: Jack's voice and hers, in scraps, fighting. The sounds lit up his nerves like neon, and the signs read *fit.* When he touched the wall, they stopped.

Just keep on walkin. At the top of the stairs, pale minnows of light from the street dove through the front windows, shimmered down the hall, and nosed at the wall of the room where he stood.

That same light, he minded, grey as an old board. That old Arkansas house was full of it. He had broken out of the Home and come to find them in the old house where they'd been staying, and they'd already left for the city without leaving him word. Or they'd sent word and nobody told him. Or they'd already lost the address of the Home.

It was cold. He slept that night in the lone house with the wind whooping around it and he could hear the owl in the rafters and the mice in the corners and the blacksnake roping up under the floor so he knew they'd been gone for days or weeks already, time enough for the animals to move back in.

And in the morning he bound up his blanket together with the crackers he'd carried from the Home (it wasn't really a home: he knew what it was) and the tin of Vienna sausage he'd found in the house, and stepped out into the porch. In the yard stood a crowd of ripe yellow-green sunflowers, twenty at least, their petals all burnt and twisted. Grass and morning glories had choked off some of them at the edge of the patch, but most were as tall as the eaves of the house and their morning shadows stretched across him. Their stalks crooked downward at the neck and their dark seedy faces hung down toward the earth. But the leaves lifted from the stalks like palms. He looked at them for a moment, with their blankety shadow and their smell of seed, the hanging heads and the uplifted leaves, then started walking: for Cincinnati, because that was how they went, house to house, country to city. And back.

In the country there were houses enough, because of all the

people that had left. And nobody cared much if you used them. And when the work there was gone and the bad luck came, they'd move on to another. And always, on the first night, there would be snakes and birds and small animals and maybe a dog, lean and studded with ticks. The dogs were a bad sign to Jack. He always said that in Arkansas even the dogs either got out or tried to kill themselves.

But that aint true. He knew. A dog would trot right out in front of a truck and you could see how skinny was its ribs and maybe you could even see the ragged parts of his ears. And he'd look like he was laying up to go right under the truck wheels, and you'd see him go under the wheels for sure, head ducked down low and his eyes winced shut, and you'd wait to hear the thump against your feet and to feel the wheels shake over him. But nothing would happen. You'd pass over where he had to be and you'd look back and there he'd be at the side of the road, tongue out, panting, looking at your tail-lights.

That was a strange thing. That was hanging on. That was Arkansas.

But Jack never wanted any part of it. More and more he wanted to stay in Cincinnati where he could work the scrap metal and fix up old cars, play guitar for his friends he found in bars, have a TV, and collect his check.

So that's why he figured they'd gone to Cincinnati. Anyway, there was nothing else to try. So he started to walk. People talked about him for it later. "You mean you didn't even hitch?" was what they usually asked. He'd just walked, mostly along the side of the highways, stopping at stores to ask directions or steal some food. And when he got to Cincinnati, he just stopped at the first police station he came to and asked them where Jack and Mae and all his brothers and Jack's LittleJack and the babies all were and they passed him from station to station til he found the one where they said, "Them? Yeah we know them. Are you another one?" And then he came to their door and said, "Here's your blanket you left behind."

And his mother put her shocked hand to her mouth and Jack just turned to the wall and shook his head.

Right here. This house. Before we got put out. That was even before John came to stay, the only scattered brother he hadn't hardly known, that he'd only seen once before, in that house in

133

Arkansas before the County sent him to the Home, in that house that was filled like a well with grey light before night fell on him lonesome with the owl and the mice and the blacksnake.

Now, by that same greysilver light he found the room where he remembered the fire escape, then he looked for the window. They had already put the glasses in, so he had to find the latch, release it, shove up the window, and let himself out onto the iron. The iron rang like a bucket when he stepped.

4. Mae

Pure white, long-haired naked Jesus, head, shoulders, and chest, looked down in a marble stare from his pedestal onto dead lumpy Earl in the grey suit they'd bought him. From her chair of honor at the side of the room she watched the full circle around Earl. At the head was Jesus, and from shoulder to leg stood her sister and her boys from down in Arkansas, at his foot was her sister's old man, the preacher, stiff as a new dollar. Behind the casket blared the ranks of empty wicker flower horns in their iron stands. The flower truck was outside, and Jack was arguing with the flower man over some way Jack could prove that he was going to pay. Not a flower til he did.

Her sister, at the shoulder of the casket, shook her mourning head and said, "It looks just like him." It didn't.

She remembered, *I never yet looked at a casket where it didn't look like the dead chest was breathin, slow and slight.*

But Earl's chest looked like they had stuck a barrel up in under his shirt. The collar rode up high on his neck, to hide the marks, and the breast of his shirt was all stretched and starched and puffed up around the collar, so that it looked like there wasn't even a neck there at all and that they'd gone ahead and cut him apart and taken his head off and fooled with it to see what was in it and then laid it at the end of whatever thing they had for his chest. And they'd done the same thing with his hands: picked them apart and laid them clean and limp and waxy like plastic apples on top of it. If they were his hands at all.

Head and hands. Bits and pieces. *They must of gone ahead and cut him up anyways. I told em they couldn't and I wouldn't sign the paper. But they might of gone ahead. They're like that. They don't really care what you want. If they really wanted the cause of*

134

his death, they'd of cut him up whether I wanted it or not.

Cause of death. They could tell as good as I could what was his cause of death. They could see him a-hangin there like a side of beef. They wanted to know if he was under the influence of drugs. Of course he was, cause he always took em for his fits.

Cause of death. Now if they want to know what caused him to want to go and hang himself, they'll have a good question, one that'll not be answered by cutting him apart. And even myself, turning him over and prodding at him in my mind, I can't come to no answer. I can't come to no answer. But how do I live with a question like that?

It's hard, because now he's deader than any of them ever were, his brothers that I lost in Arkansas when they drowned or my one sister, or my father, or all those cousins in that fire. Bits and pieces, that's all he looks like. Powder on his face. His hair all slick and combed wrong. And his hands all red and waxy and clean like he'd never worked on a car before or a bike before like he always did. The only thing that looks like him at all is the turn at the corner of his mouth and the raised-up place at the side of his eye. And that was probably an accident by the funeral man that dressed him up for this thing.

Those hands are what's deadest. He always had dirt in his hands ground right in where you could see every line in them cause he never could wash it out, not even to go to school. Those hands don't look like his hands. They look like spare hands the same size and shape that they had a-layin around and they put on the ends of his arms because they couldn't clean the grease out of his real ones nor break the claw out of them.

I've heard about how them people work, how they break bones and use spare parts to make people look like what they think they ought to look like. Just about like Jack does with them cars.

Now the way the old people done it, they never left a body alone til they buried it. They stayed right with it. If we could of done that, they'd of never cut him up and he'd not look so dead now that I can't think straight about him. But them cops just took him away like he was theirs and them people went and tore him up.

And that's why I can't get him settled in my mind. He's so dead and destroyed I can't find him no more, at least nothin of him that I can understand. I look at Lloyd and I can see him sittin there a-

135

*foldin his hands and pullin them apart and lookin at the floor and
I know he's sorrowful and lonesome for Earl and he's hurt. But at
least he's settled in his mind. He's got a notion it was some boys
from over on Vine Street and he's gonna pick a fight with em
before another couple days. But he's settled in his mind, for better
or worse.*

*But I'm not. I can't settle it, not how he died nor why he died nor
nothin.*

*It might be them pills they give me. They said that after I seen
Earl bein put away in that box I started to moan and cry and knock
about on people and the walls of that dead house and wrap myself
together like there was something ugly being born out of me right
then and there. I don't remember that. What I remember feeling is
like the world had opened me up like a blanket and filled me up
with stones and sewed me up over em.*

*So they say they took me over to the clinic and that doctor gave
me a fistful of pills and I took em and went quiet as a tree, that's
how dead I was for that time. Most dead bodies is like that, you
know, like a tree, when you go see them at a funeral. You see them
almost like they was movin, almost like a tree moves in a slow
wind. And that's how you think of them, like a tree, because a tree
moves and changes real slow, and even a dead body changes. It
rots, and becomes earth, and new plants and trees feed out of it.
You don't think about it much, but it happens, and that
knowledge is there in your mind. But when a body is so dead and
destroyed that it won't even seem to move, like it's plastic or a
stone, then there's something that aint right.*

Someone shifted in a folding chair and its wooden slats popped
into their new place.

*You could hear the dead branches pop in the wind high up in
the trees the night John was born. I was just a girl when I first
married. My man was a logger and he used to go out with a crew for
days at a time and leave me alone with that cabin and that creek
and all those black trees. I didn't mind it. I didn't care about
anything back then. I could handle myself pretty good and I used
to spend all the time I could up in the woods. And when I was
about to have my first, he left me to go out with the loggers, cause I
didn't think I was due yet. But it started right away that night. And
we lived, you see, all by ourselves up a hollar and not even a neighbor for a mile. But there was an old woman used to pass us. Hadn't*

136

never said a word ever. And she never did. She heard me a-screamin with the child for someone to come and she came into the cabin and she helped me to birth it without hardly sayin a word. And when it was done she just washed up the baby and put it to bed and cooked up a lot of food for me to eat til I got better, and she left.

That was John.

After John there were two more, but they died and then my first man died and I went sort of wild, you see. I had moved back with my mother where I kind of left John and I started ridin of a night with these boys and, you know, stayin out of a night. And one of those boys was Jack. Well, Jack took me to the city for him to find work, then back to the country to find work, then to the city and back to the country, and then he hurt his back and nobody wouldn't hire him and that left him with just the Social Security and whatever he could make tradin cars, and we'd head back and forth from the city to the country, back and forth, wherever things looked better. And all that time I been havin babies pretty regular. And some of em's been placed, here and there, cause of what the Welfare said. Or they'd be placed awhile and we'd pick em back up. Or they'd run away, as Earl done, and come find us.

And I don't know why they'd ever want to come find us, cause we never was much good to em. Like right now, these new babies take up all of my time so I can't do nothin for these boys and they run the streets wild as deer. And Jack, he don't care nothin about em anyway except when he needs em to work or when they get in trouble. And then he'll just shake his head and say it's one damn thing after another.

And when Earl come to the house I felt awful bad, cause I'd sort of hoped he'd stay at that Home, cause he always was the most trouble of em all, cause he'd always be gettin picked on and fightin back, and cause he had those fits. Those awful turnin-blue fits. And it hurt him that I felt bad, cause he knew. I couldn't hide it. And neither could he. He come to the door this last time with that blanket rolled up under his arm just a-grinnin and waitin for somebody to welcome him in. And when nobody said nothin to him and I couldn't say nothin and Jack just shook his head, I watched that grin lose all its heart til he had to prop it up from inside like a coathanger does a coat.

That was that same house where he hung hisself that we was livin in then. The same house.

And after that I tried to care about him, but these babies is my main worry and it seemed like I never had the time. Lloyd took up with him and that colored boy Lonnie and they all run together, but they aint much better than Earl except that they don't have fits.

Now Earl worked with Jack on them cars, and he was learnin pretty good there, but not fast enough for Jack. Earl would always hand him the wrong tool. Or he'd let all the oil pour out onto the street instead of catching it in the bucket. Or he'd let the car down off the jack before he got the tire back on. Or he'd start the motor when Jack had his hand down in it. Lord that'd make Jack mad. But he was a-learnin some.

He was a-learnin at school too. That Welfare lady said he could stay here with us as long as he went to school, and he wanted to stay and not be sent off again, so he went ever day and got in a fight ever day. Him and Lloyd. The coloreds'd talk about his clothes and he wouldn't like it. But he was a-tryin to learn. They'd give him books to read and he'd bring em home and he'd try to read em till the sweat'd pour off his face like rain off a rock. And he never ever sweat when he was a-workin.

And I believe they made his fits worse, cause the doctor told him if he felt a fit comin on he should go in a quiet corner and read. Well, he'd try one place and the babies'd be cryin. And he'd try another and Jack'd be a-playin the guitar and he wouldn't want him around. And he'd try another and Lloyd and Little Jack would be havin a fight. And the next thing you know he'd be flyin out of the house with his tongue hangin out his face and we'd hear from all the neighbors that he was rollin in the street and turnin blue.

But John, he would try to teach him what he could when he was around. He'd show him how to use his tools and to be careful with his work. He'd show him how you don't strip the threads or snap a bolt. Or how you pull an axle with a tow-chain.

Lord I wish he could of stayed by him. But he had to go. And I can't blame him. It's too much out of his life to try to live his own life and make Earl's straight too, especially when he's got school, Jack, the police and every law they got, doctors, the welfare, half the neighborhood, thirteen specialists, a landlord, that gang of boys from Vine Street, and ever time you turn around some new bunch of enemies against him. It's just too much. Too much for me. Too much for John.

You could hear the dead branches pop in the wind when John was born. It was that lonesome. But when Earl was born you could hear loudspeakers and babies and sirens and nurses and Jack cussin at everone in sight. Because I had started to get my pains and I said to Jack, I need to get to the hospital now, and he went out to get the car started and it wouldn't start, so he come a-stormin in sayin it wouldn't start and I started to scream with some of the pains and I said, Can't we take a cab? And he said he didn't have the fare and would I quit aggervatin him cause it wasn't even his baby anyway, not this one. Which it wasn't. I wasn't entirely settled down with Jack then. Well, finally he borrowed a car to take me up there, but they wouldn't take me in there because he didn't have money nor a medical card either, so he got mad and threatened to pull out his gun, and they called the police right then and they come a-tearin up and they're ready to arrest him and me both but I started to havin Earl right then, right there on those old hard benches. And then they started to call for the doctor and the nurses and the stretchers to take me to a room, and I told em to stay away. They didn't want to help me before they aint agonna help me now, and by God I had that baby right there in the next half hour holdin a pocketknife in my hand for any cop or nurse or anybody else that'd try to move me out of there. And my cousin that was with me tied off the cord and all and I went out of there carryin that baby myself.

And maybe I shouldn't have been so proud and I should of let em take care of me and him. They say a baby can be damaged if it don't get the right care at first. And Earl got damaged somewhere. He got damaged ever time he turned around.

A new set of mourners came into the room. She didn't look up. She could tell by their shadows that they crossed stiffly in front of her to the center of the room, whispering, leaning at each other like doves.

They'll be around to tell me in a minute: How sorry they are; it looks just like him. It don't. It looks like something dead, and Earl was never dead til now. And now he's so dead and damaged I can't never get him back or begin again on him or have any hope but for the babies that they might not go through the same godawful thing.

And I guess that's the only good reason to think on a dead person, cause he's either with Jesus or he aint, and there sure aint anything I can do about it now. But there's a lesson to be learned for those that's left behind. And if I could find an easy lesson, I'd be glad of it, for Earl's so dead and destroyed to me now it's like they made him into one of them white stone statues.

The new mourners paused in their murmuring. She could sense them ready to turn, to come to her, to say the words she had already heard, and she thought *Oh God why does Earl have to be so dead?* Every sight and every sound become a rolling memory: The popping of the chairs, the empty horns, the murmuring and wallpaper were trees and old women, wind up a hollar, and battered suitcases.

5. Earl

Keep your eye on that moon.

The full white round of it had leaped free of the wall and it spun toward the black peak of the sky.

You don't want to miss the time, he thought. He pulled on the belt again, to test again. *It's a damn good knot,* he thought. *It'll hold. I had to work a-while to learn that knot. You have to work to learn any good thing: to work with tools or play music or read a book. They don't even know I could learn something like that. They don't know I been learnin. There's a lot they don't know.*

They'll learn. But they'll have to work at it. My work's done.

6. John

It's a thing we'll never know the end of, he thought. *Not with so many pieces and odd springs to it. What could be the end to it?*

They said the thing that set him off like that was what happened when he was trying to put that universal joint back in for Jack. He spilled that little cap that holds all those small pencil-shape bearings that stand around the inside of the cap, one against another. If you spill them ever, you have a time putting them back in, cause they want to slip and slant and fall inward and pick up grit, and even once you've got em all lined up just right but for the last one, it'll all go out again, or three of em'll stick to your fingers and pull the rest loose and you're back where you started. But it can be done if you stay with it. And Earl was the kind to stay with it if they'd let him. But they say that Jack had jumped all over him and

140

slapped him into the street with Mae standin in the door and he turned on her right away and dared her to say something about her retarded greasy-fingered dragass son that couldn't keep his fingers to hisself. Dared her. And she didn't say a word. Couldn't. What could she say?

That could of been it. Earl wouldn't of cared what she said, even if it was only to cuss Jack back. But she didn't say anything. That would hurt. It would be like givin up and sayin that all that Jack had said was true and Earl wasn't nothin more to her but more trouble on top of what she already had.

You can take these pieces, though. They're little brassy lookin things shaped about like a sausage. You can take em and pick em out of whatever grit they're scattered into and clean em off with a piece of cloth and began to rank em back into that cap. Just add a little grease cause they'll burn out if they're dry and the grease helps hold em in. You just take em one by one. Use the tip of a knife if your finger's too thick, and rank em up, one by one, one against the other, til you've got that last one. That's where you got to be careful cause it fits in there snug and it'll want to buckle the others out when you go to push on it. So you put your fingers of one hand, as many as you can get in there, against the bearings, and you push on that last one with a finger from your other hand. And it'll pop in there tighter than a banjo head.

Just about anything can be pieced together. If you can get to work on it right.

7. Earl

Watch that moon.

Once I'm still, I'll be in a plumb line to the earth and a plumb line to the moon, like a cord between the two. In the school, the teacher taught how years and years ago, older than the oldest man, the moon was a piece of the earth. But it broke off and spun loose and now it runs around the earth, all through the sky, never no closer, but never no further either.

My runnin's over. No closer, but no further either.
Watch that moon.

Check the knot. The rabbit, up, around, back down in the hole. It'll hold.
My hands are full of sweat.

He began to be afraid of them, that they would deny him, grab for the iron and not let go til the right time had passed.

What can I do with em?
They were like threats. They wanted one last touch, they told him, one last touch of the iron. Traitors.

Watch that moon.
That moon!

He leaped, higher than he needed to, so that as he leaped the belt caught him short and jerked him back down, thinking as he fell: Just this and then a blank.

But no blank: The belt jerked him short and stung his face and stopped his blood and caught him in a deep drowning that he could no way swim out of. He spun around once: streetlight, courtlight, moon. Breathe, he demanded. But his breath was in a bottle that he could not break. Streetlight. Courtlight.

My hands, he thought. *Reach for the knot.*
He tried to reach across his chest, but the blood had spoiled in his shoulders, so he tried from the back.

Moon.
His hands.